THE PREMONITION

Nostradamus lives . . . in his descendant Michael Dartson. On a journey to the homes of his ancestors, a strangely bewitching woman shows him that the past is alive. Michael must experience the most traumatic moments of his forefathers' lives — rape, cannibalism, unspeakable violence. His infamous ancestor has set some terrible plan in motion — and Michael is only an instrument. The time is near. The horrors of the past are nothing compared to the evils of the future . . .

DREW LAUNAY

THE
PREMONITION

Complete and Unabridged

LINFORD
Leicester

First published in Great Britain

First Linford Edition
published 2010

This book was originally published in Great
Britain as *Premonitions of an Inherited Mind.*

British Library CIP Data

Launay, Drew, *1930 –*
    The premonition. - -
    (Linford mystery library)
    1. Nostradamus, *1503 – 1566-* -Fiction.
    2. Horror tales. 3. Large type books.
    I. Title II. Series
    823.9'14–dc22

ISBN 978–1–44480–458–4

Central Park, New York.

11:30 on the morning of March 3rd Michael Dartson was taking a last walk before returning to his apartment on East 76th Street to collect his hand luggage and go to the airport.

He stopped, closed his eyes and, for a moment, turned his face to the sun, then he heard the woman's voice quite distinctly.

'Don't touch that package, for God's sake don't touch it!'

He felt an area of the ground around him shudder, then fearful screams of panic enveloped him.

Ten days later it happened.

1

The Piccadilly Circus subway station serves two tube lines in the centre of London's underground transport network. It is a complex of passenger platforms on different levels, well below ground, linked by tunnelways reached by numerous escalators.

At 5:45 on Monday, 13th March, Norma Dartson, unable to get a taxi in Regent Street after a tiring afternoon's shopping, joined the rush hour commuters going down the Piccadilly tube.

Holding tightly onto her handbag and gripping the top of her mink coat, she battled to get a ticket and, once through the automatic barrier machines, relaxed a little on the steps of the descending escalator, calculating that within twenty minutes or so she would be back above ground in the fresher Knightsbridge air, and soon sitting down for a hotel tea with her daughter Sarah.

As the escalator reached the bottom hallway and she was checking the indications to the various destinations, she became aware of a confusion to her right. Amid the mass of people hurrying in various directions, a group were trying to avoid something on the floor.

It was a package, neatly wrapped in brown paper, and tied with white string.

Then she saw a woman stoop to pick it up.

There was a blinding flash of blue and white light, followed by a thunderous blast.

Norma felt herself showered with icy water which then gave off unbearable heat. Putting her hand up to her face to protect it, she felt it to be sticky and she tasted blood.

All around her was black, people were screaming, bellowing in terror, there was a massive surge against her and she crumpled to the ground, her legs folding under her, trapped painfully by her own weight.

As she blindly struggled to free herself, she thought of her handbag, her gold wrist-watch, the state of her coat, felt the agony of a sharp heel digging into her neck, then to her horror she realized she was choking.

Blood, acrid fumes filled her mouth and nose, she gasped for air. Pressing down on her was a body and then she realized that her hand was trapped by something metallic which was being pushed towards her.

Was it possible that she would be crushed? That she would die?

People would come to the rescue, people always did. There had been an explosion, an accident, the lights had gone out, understandably, all she had to do was remain calm, bear with the agony of her pinioned leg, not worry that she could no longer feel her hand. But then another surge crushed in on her and this time she felt a much deeper pain right in the centre of her stomach. She coughed, the blood came up from deep within her, and she let go, trying to sense it dribbling from her mouth. She tried to feel the edge of her teeth with her tongue . . .

Oh God! Her free hand was there

touching her top lip, but there was no jaw . . .

She was a corpse, a mutilated body, a consciousness hanging onto life.

And with her next breath, it ended.

★　★　★

Michael Dartson was enjoying that peace of mind and tranquillity many people strive for over a lifetime, but seldom find. At forty-eight it seemed he had arrived. He had a happy marriage, financial success, freedom of movement, total independence and even the ear of many in power.

Having breakfast, on the first-floor balcony of his newly acquired four-storey villa in the South of France, he looked beyond the garden's magnificent palm trees at the sparkling blue Mediterranean, knowing he had no appointments, no meetings, that no one was expecting anything of him except perhaps Norma who would prefer to find the house tidier than it was when she got back.

She had gone to London to see Sarah

and buy a new wardrobe for the new life; she would be away another three days, ample time for him to unpack all the tea chests, sort out the books and the antiques, arrange the furniture and make the all-important decisions about which paintings should hang where.

After the tragedy of eight months ago when Sarah's husband, David, had been killed, followed by the problems of deciding to sell up the New York business consultancy and set up another in Europe, he deserved the rest.

He hoped Norma would be able to persuade Sarah to come down and have her expected baby locally; it would be preferable for her to be with her mother, though no doubt David's parents would want the baby to be born in their home, which would mean that Norma would worry, would fly back and forth to England to help and they wouldn't be able to settle down for God knew how long.

He had managed to push business thoughts to the back of his mind since moving into the villa, but he expected that after a few more days he would feel the need to start ringing up contacts again. A glance at the morning's paper had already suggested a number of profitable moves for some of his clients who had money to invest in Europe. Though he had promised Norma to have at least one month's holiday, a month was a long time to remain dormant and he was looking forward to just getting into the car and driving across the borders to Geneva and Milan, and up to Paris, without the tedious business of booking flights and waiting at airports.

Selfish sentiments perhaps, but the move had partly been hurried up to be closer to Sarah when her time came. Best of course if she moved down here completely. There was certainly enough room.

The telephone rang, reminding him again that the engineers had still not come to fix the extensions.

He crossed the bedroom, went slowly down the main stairs, squeezed past the packing cases in the main hall, and went into the study.

The telephone was on the floor next to

the leather couch he had acquired from the previous owners, along with other useful pieces of furniture.

He sat down and picked up the receiver.

'Cagnes trente sept, douze, quarante huit,' he said, amused by his own accent.

'Daddy? It's Sarah.' The girlish voice was tense and much younger than its twenty-one years.

'Sarah.'

'Daddy, I've got terrible news. There's been an accident . . . '

He heard the explanation.

A bomb in the Piccadilly underground last night.

She hadn't started worrying 'till about seven, and then heard the news on the radio. After that she'd known. She hadn't rung him until confirmation had come through from the police, just now. Norma's handbag had been found, her wrist-watch. Seventy people had died, over a hundred were injured.

'I'll catch the first 'plane,' he said. 'I'll ring back to tell you which flight as soon as I can.'

Norma dead. David, now Norma.

Sarah met him at Heathrow Airport. She was wearing a long flowered dress, flaring out from above the waist, and he didn't take in its significance till they hugged each other and he felt the hardness of her stomach.

'It'll be a girl, she'll be a Pisces,' she said bravely, trying to hold back the tears.

'You can let go now Sarah, relax a little.'

'Not here. Not with so many people around. Can we take a taxi?'

'Of course.'

As soon as they got in the taxi she started crying, uncontrollably, burying her face in his coat as he hugged her, patted her, tried to console her.

'The terrible thing is,' she said between breaths, 'the terrible thing is that I knew it was going to happen, like I knew it would happen to David.'

He had never indulged her in her fantasies. Never. Neither he nor Norma had ever openly shown surprise at her predictions, though some of them in the past had been astonishing.

'About ten days ago I heard voices shouting to someone not to touch something, then the floor shuddered as though I was on a moving staircase which had suddenly come to a stop.'

He said nothing at all but just looked out of the window at the passing scenery. It was raining, a deadly March evening in London.

'A few days before David had the crash I had a similar experience, the sensation that his burnt body was next to me in bed . . . ' She sat up and took a small handkerchief from her coat pocket and dabbed her eyes. 'It's so sad that neither of them will see the baby.'

He took her hand in his and squeezed it hard. He didn't want her to start crying again. He didn't want to think of things like that at all. He had been through it enough times in his head ever since her call; waiting at the airport, sitting in the 'plane, he'd had plenty of time to think of what the future could have been and what it was going to be now.

The taxi turned down a small street

and stopped outside the hotel, and Sarah dabbed her eyes again, took a compact from her handbag and had a quick look at her swollen eyes.

'Melanie mustn't see me like this,' she said.

'Who's Melanie?'

'A friend. Came to keep me company. She's been wonderful.'

Melanie opened the front door of the hotel suite. She had freckles, looked about sixteen, had gingery hair, strange grey eyes, and seemed terrified of everything.

She was obviously efficient, had written down the calls that had come in since Sarah had left to meet him at the airport, and even handed him the keys to the room she had booked across the corridor.

'Six 'phone calls, two callers. The police would like one of you to go to the hospital to identify the body as soon as possible, two funeral directors have offered their services, David's mother rang to ask how you were again, and the *Evening Standard* and *Evening News* wanted to talk to you.'

'Who were the callers?'

'The same. *Evening Standard* and *Evening News*.'

'What did you say?' Sarah asked, slumping down in a chair, clearly exhausted.

'I told them to mind their own business, which is why they came round.'

'Where are you from?' Michael asked her. She had an American accent.

'Virginia, originally. But I've been living in London some time.'

'Have you the name of those funeral directors?'

'Yes. Here. I wrote them down.'

He looked at the names, the telephone numbers.

'I'll ring them tomorrow,' he said, more to himself than anybody.

'What are you going to do with . . . her?' Sarah asked.

'I want her buried in the cemetery at Cagnes. I want to feel she's near. She liked Cagnes, was looking forward . . . '

'I also got you some tranquillizers,' Melanie said cheerfully before his thoughts could get the better of them all. 'Went round to the doctor's surgery and explained.

11

I think you should both take one.'

'Thanks,' Michael said, grateful. 'I'll take one tonight when I go to bed.'

* * *

He left Sarah in Melanie's capable hands and took a taxi to the Hospital.

A uniformed policeman had a check list and requested that he should follow him down to the basement mortuary.

It was a large refrigerated room with bodies under white sheets on trolleys, thirty or so, well spaced out. A hospital official in a white coat joined them.

'Who is it?' he asked the officer.

'Mr. Dartson. His wife. Number 8.'

'Oh yes . . . '

The man was tired, lines of weariness creased a strained apologetic smile around his mouth.

'Do you remember any birthmark or notable scar?' he asked. 'It's less distressing to look at a limb or an area of the body.'

Michael couldn't remember any scars, couldn't remember anything about her.

'Her appendix?' he suggested after a while.

'I'm afraid not. Too many people . . . '

'She had a mole under her right breast, quite a large one, egg shaped, about a third of an inch long.'

The doctor carefully lifted the middle of the white sheet and exposed Norma's body. The arm was bruised, blue, and he instantly recognized her hand, the index finger with the small band-aid where she had cut herself opening a tin of anchovies when they were having their first snack in the empty villa.

The fingers were rigid.

The man uncovered her breasts. He saw the mole.

'That's all that's necessary,' he said.

'Was her face damaged?' Michael asked.

'It's best not to look,' the doctor said, and somehow turned him away and led him out of the room.

★ ★ ★

After a solemn meal in their hotel suite that evening, Melanie saying nothing,

13

Sarah hardly eating, they sat down to watch television until the newscaster started on the disaster story.

He got up and switched it off.

He was tired, so he excused himself and left the girls alone to go to his room, thankful that Melanie was there occupying Norma's bed next to Sarah.

He wanted to ignore what Sarah had said about her premonition, but of course he couldn't.

For the second time now he had had the same experience as her, and that was unexplainable.

He undressed and got into bed and lay there with his eyes wide open in the dark; then he decided not to risk the exhaustion of a sleepless night, so got up again to take one of Melanie's tranquillizers.

It had been in a similar hotel bedroom that he'd had the premonition of David's death, in Boston. He'd gone to bed early, and as he'd pulled the sheets up over his shoulders, for a fraction of a second he'd felt he was not alone, that there was someone in the bed with him. He'd eased himself away from the feeling and suddenly had smelt the repugnant odour of burnt skin and hair. It instantly reminded him of a motor accident he had witnessed on a highway outside New York when several cars had collided and one had caught fire. The driver, burning like a torch, had collapsed on the tarmac right in front of him and he had helped put out the flames with his jacket. This smell had been exactly the same.

He'd reached out in the dark, found the overhead bed lamp and switched it on.

There had been nothing, no one. The smell had gone. So he'd switched the light off again and thought no more about it.

The next day he'd learned that David had been killed in a 'plane crash, burnt alive in the cockpit of the aircraft he was testing.

2

'I have to tell you now, Daddy,' Sarah said suddenly, as she opened her small suitcase. 'The tragedies are not yet over. I'm going to have this baby, it'll be a lovely blue-eyed little girl, but I won't live through the birth.'

He was standing in the doorway of the double room on the third floor of the villa, having accepted that she much preferred sharing a room with Melanie to sleeping alone in the main guest room on the second floor as he had suggested.

Both had come down for Norma's funeral and brought enough luggage to suggest that they intended staying quite a time.

Now Sarah was making this terrible announcement.

'What makes you say that?' he asked cautiously.

'I quite simply had this dream last night when I saw myself being buried

16

next to Mummy. I can describe the cemetery for you if you want. It's rather crowded with elaborate tombs, some Italian in style, with photographs of the beloved departed. Mummy's grave is in a corner next to a rather nice archangel.'

He had been to the cemetery to see the grave; she was right, yet he knew she had never been there.

'When you've settled down a bit and changed, or whatever you want to do, I'll show you round the house,' he said, changing the subject. 'I'll be in the study downstairs. Just shout.'

And he left.

He had met Sarah and Melanie at Nice airport after flying down the day before in a private 'plane with Norma's coffin, a journey he had not expected to enjoy but which in fact had turned out to be remarkably peaceful.

Before leaving London he had tried to convince Sarah that it would be better for her to get away from England, leave her parents-in-law with whom she had been living in Suffolk, and have her baby in the better climate, and she had eventually decided to do that. He had not expected Melanie to come too, but in a way it made things a lot easier, especially if Sarah was going to be in one of her imaginative phases again.

From the age of seven she'd had nightmares, with fearful screams waking him up in the night. Himself a light sleeper, he had been the one to leap out of bed and rush to her room to find her curled up, sucking her thumb, wide awake and frightened but with that look of resignation in her eyes, accepting the inevitable.

'Are you all right?' he'd ask.

'Yes, thank you, Daddy. It was only another dream.'

Right through her school years it had continued, her reports invariably ending with the criticism that 'Sarah should learn to control her imagination.'

She had foretold tragedies before, once at the age of eleven, when a fire had gutted some stables, killing a number of horses; there had been no family connection. Then when she was seventeen she had foreseen the death of a school friend

18

who was on a skiing holiday in Mammoth Lakes.

At nineteen she had married David; not unnaturally she had forecast the wedding because she was in love with him, but they had married sooner than expected and she had gone to live on the farm in Suffolk.

Her many letters had always been happy except for the one received a week before his death. 'David is testing a new executive jet this week,' she had written, 'and I'm afraid our days of happiness together may be numbered.'

Now she was saying it was her turn?

* * *

Because of the mild weather and the brightness of the sun, they managed to get through the day of the funeral without too much sadness.

Over tea Melanie suggested that she and Sarah should take over the running of the house, which would keep them busy until the baby was due, and that made sense. He contacted a good doctor and had everything organized for her to have the child at home with a live-in nurse booked to come the moment things started happening.

He was intrigued by Melanie, fascinated by her. She was so quiet, a mouse of a girl, yet obviously with a mind very much her own.

She had stared at him during the funeral, and when he'd plucked a carnation from a wreath to throw onto the coffin as it was lowered into the grave, he had managed to control his emotion because she was watching him. In fact he remembered the funeral not as the day Norma was buried but as the day he became aware of Melanie.

One morning she brought him up breakfast and the fact that he was naked under the sheets made her blush, which made him even more aware of her femininity.

Her freckled face, her reddish hair, her large grey eyes, were all things he had noticed and enjoyed. He liked having attractive people around, but now her slim youthful body, her long legs, her long hands with short nails, made him realize that he was quite simply attracted to her.

He thanked her gruffly, heavy with sleep, and accepted the explanation of why she had brought him up breakfast at all.

'Sarah's had a restless night, so she's lying in, and I'm going to the village to buy groceries early. So here's your breakfast.'

Why complain? He was happy, had not been so content for a long time. Content, that was, when he was able to live in the present and the future and not think of the past with Norma.

The tray that Melanie had brought him was more than breakfast. A large bowl of coffee, croissants wrapped in a paper napkin, butter in a small dish, a choice of jam or marmalade in tiny separate pots, a pink rose picked from the garden in a silver egg cup: It was nearly breakfast with love.

He ate it all and eventually got up, shaved, showered, dressed and went up to see Sarah who was lying in bed looking pale and dark under the eyes.

'How are you feeling?'

'O.K. She's been kicking a bit.'

The pallid smile was still being brave. He wanted to cheer her up but didn't know how. Alone he could cope with the sadness, but with her it became a shared loss with more memories and therefore less bearable.

'The doctor's coming today,' she said. 'Melanie rang him. I hope you don't mind.'

'Why should I mind?'

'He wants to talk to you.'

'Me?'

'There's going to be a problem, Daddy. I told you.'

He wasn't going to dispute her pessimism, it would lead nowhere.

'What time is he coming?'

'Twelvish.'

'Do you want anything?'

'Nope. I'm quite happy lying here.'

When the doctor arrived Melanie met him at the front door and made the introductions. She had twice been to see him with Sarah at his consulting rooms.

'So we are to be a grandfather!' he said to Michael.

They shook hands.

He was an amiable man in his sixties, with white hair, white hands and impeccable manners; he had been recommended by the priest who had officiated at Norma's funeral because he spoke English perfectly.

'How is the patient, do you think?' Michael asked, leading the way to the elevator, a piece of machinery which everyone was surprised to see in a private house, as indeed it had surprised him when he first visited the villa.

The doctor pouted uncertainly, stopped and, in a whisper, explained, 'The child is fine, the pregnancy is fine, but your daughter has a weak heart.'

'There is cause for concern then?'

'What I may suggest is that she should have the baby in the clinic, but let me examine her first.'

'Shall we go up to the bedroom?' Melanie suggested, and she opened the elevator gates.

'Is it expensive to run?' the doctor

23

asked, fascinated by the elevator.

'Only if it breaks down, apparently. I don't use it much.'

'But for Madame Sarah it is ideal.'

Michael closed the outside gate for them and watched the cage ascending. It had been a major attraction when he'd thought of buying the place. Not everyone had an elevator they could call their own.

He sat down alone in the drawing room and picked up the *Herald Tribune*.

The headlines didn't interest him. Nothing interested him. He was worried by what the doctor had said. Norma had had a weak heart but hadn't had any complications when Sarah was born.

A number of things were beginning to build up into a pattern he didn't want to face, with Sarah's premonitions and his own, not that he had had visions of Sarah being buried or anything like that. In fact his mind had been quite clear recently. They were all depressed because of Norma's death. He should not start imagining things which could not be logically explained. That Sarah was flirting with the occult, apparently recording her dreams with Melanie, was perhaps a safety valve for which he should be grateful. Under similar stress many expectant mothers might well have reacted more strongly.

He heard voices upstairs, the examination was over, the elevator was on its way down. He went to meet the doctor.

'A little aperitif?' he suggested.

'Un petit whisky. But really petit.'

'How is she?' Michael asked.

'I think it would be wise for her to come in this evening. She is very tense, trying hard not to show it. I would like her to be under mild sedation where we can keep an eye on her.'

'You're really worried, aren't you?'

'She believes she is going to have a bad time, but won't say why,' the doctor explained. 'She talks as though she were not going to be there to look after the baby.'

'She's always been pessimistic. Her husband died eight months ago, as you know, then her mother. It is understandable. Has the shock caused problems?'

'Not directly. But I think we should watch her after the baby is born. There is always post-natal depression, and she is already at a low level. But her friend is good for her, a great calming influence. Extraordinary eyes she has, cette petite.'

* * *

The drive back from the clinic with Melanie, after settling Sarah in, was taxing on his nerves. He thanked God that he had had the presence of mind to invite friends round for coffee.

Melanie sat next to him, quite erect, alert of eye, not moving her head to look at the scenery. He wished she would unwind.

'I've invited some friends round for coffee; he's an artist from New York, she's Danish. Would you like to join us?'

'Raulk?' she asked, turning. 'The man who painted those tortuous canvases you have in the penthouse sitting room?'

'Yes. Don't you like them?'

'It would be interesting to meet him.'

She glanced at him and smiled, a very

26

sweet, nearly sensuous smile.

'You invited them so that your mind would be occupied this evening, didn't you?'

'Yes,' he admitted. Perceptive of her.

'Are you afraid something is going to happen to Sarah?'

'I'm afraid she thinks something is going to happen to her, and I don't know how to help.'

'She needs no help. She's prepared.'

'You really believe something is going to happen?'

'Yes. Don't you?'

'No,' he said emphatically.

'Then you're deceiving yourself. You're even more clairvoyant than she is. You're only blind to your own powers because you're inhibited. But you'll learn.'

They had reached the house. He turned into the drive and stopped the car just short of the garage.

He didn't say anything, but just got out and walked away.

★ ★ ★

Raulk and Sigrid arrived three-quarters of an hour late, for which he was grateful. It gave him time to relax and have a couple of drinks before coping with the inevitable commiserations. They were the first mutual friends of his and Norma's that he was going to see since her death. It was through them that they had first come to Cagnes, fallen in love with the area and bought the villa.

Raulk, in jeans, black T-shirt and tetchy mood, threatened to be difficult; he was never an easy guest, but when he saw Melanie he changed his colours so rapidly that Sigrid winked. It seemed they were in for an evening of him exercising his charms on Melanie.

Michael showed them around the house which they had visited when it was empty. Now, with most of the New York furniture in place and some of the curtains up it looked lived in, if not too tidy.

He took them up to the penthouse in the elevator. Raulk was like a little boy, enjoying the ride, though he didn't approve of the mirrors on the sides and ceiling, thinking them vulgar. Melanie loved them and thought them luxuriously theatrical.

They settled down in the top living room, newly furnished in blue and white, with the ceiling-to-floor panoramic window overlooking the town and the sea beyond, and the walls graced by Raulk's huge canvases.

He was flattered by Melanie's description of his work, and liked the fact that she didn't feel at ease with the paintings.

'What do you do when you're not looking after Sarah and her father?' he asked.

'I'm a researcher.'

'Of what?'

'Anything that comes up and pays. I've worked for newspapers and market research companies, advertising agencies and in public relations. Right now I'm into psychic phenomena, for myself.'

'What sort of phenomena?' Sigrid asked.

'Every sort. From extra-sensory perception to astral projection.'

'Are you psychic yourself?' Raulk

asked, a trifle mockingly.

'Yes.'

'In what way?'

Melanie stared at Raulk for a considerable time in silence, and he stared back. They held each other's gaze like two cats across a roof.

'The identity disc you're wearing round your neck belonged to your brother who was killed in Vietnam,' Melanie said slowly. 'If I can hold it in my hand I'll tell you more about how it happened.'

Sigrid went white, not at what had been said so much as at Raulk's reaction, his obvious incredulity. Melanie might have spotted a disc under his T-shirt, but in no way could she have known what it was.

Raulk undid the catch at the back of the chain and handed her the aluminium dog-tag.

Melanie held it in the palm of her right hand and closed her eyes, then fell back on her seat like a rag doll, both arms outstretched.

They watched her fingering the disc, running her thumb over the surface. Then she suddenly opened her eyes.

'The indentations are teeth marks. His own. He often put the disc in his mouth and bit on it. He was biting on it when he died.'

'How did he die?' Raulk asked, sitting up now, tense, wanting to know.

'He was very proud, wasn't he? I'm sensing very strongly that I shouldn't tell you.' She paused, then put the disc down very carefully on the glass coffee table as though she no longer wanted to hold it. 'He was suffering from dysentery. He had the disc in his mouth; he was in pain, and was crouching when he was shot.'

'Oh God!' Sigrid cried out, horrified, 'he was having a shit?'

The disc sprang off the table of its own accord and fell on the floor.

Raulk lashed out at Sigrid and hit her across the mouth with the back of his hand, hardly aware of what he was doing, a reflex action as though in self-defence.

Sigrid stifled a scream. It hurt, but it stunned her more, and she apologized immediately.

'I wasn't laughing at him . . . I was . . . '

'But you were! You were! That's exactly what you were doing and that's exactly what he feared!' Raulk shouted at her. 'He feared ridicule more than anything.'

Michael straightened up and looked at the disc on the floor, and Melanie smiled.

'It can be explained by electrical impulses set up between Raulk and myself because we're both tense,' she said.

'But that's not your explanation?' Raulk said.

'No. My explanation is that Dermot had time to think before he died, and that his thoughts were entirely centred on how much people would laugh when they heard what had happened.'

'How did you know his name?' Sigrid asked, having recovered.

'It's on the dog-tag,' Melanie said simply.

At least she was honest.

Secretly Michael was pleased that his guest had been impressed. It was of course a story that no one could possibly check on; Melanie had probably made it up, was a practised faker who would be very acceptable at parties, but unfortunately might be a bad influence on Sarah.

She sat up and turned to look at him.

'I'm not a bad influence on Sarah,' she said. 'I've helped her a great deal, like I will help you. And you should prepare yourself for bad news very soon.'

She got slowly to her feet, walked over to the window and stared out at the darkness. 'Very soon,' she repeated. And the new extension telephone behind him rang.

She handed him the receiver.

'Monsieur Dartson? C'est Docteur Foche. Il y a une complication . . . we may have to operate, do you think you could come here as quickly as possible?'

'Of course.'

He put the receiver down and looked at Raulk, Sigrid, at Melanie, uncertain what to do.

'You go. I'll stay here with them,' she said as though she knew what had happened.

He didn't hesitate, but apologized, thanked her and left.

How could she have known? Telepathy?

Some communication she had worked out with Sarah? It was more than that.

He could somehow accept that she knew, because he knew. It wasn't anything definite, it wasn't an abysmal depression, a feeling of hopelessness, it was nothing like that. It was just a knowledge, a known fact which he had been expecting ever since Sarah had first mentioned it.

When he eventually reached the clinic the receptionist's expression confirmed it all. It was in the eyes, the fear of having to hurt him, of having to cope with possible collapse.

Nervously she picked up an internal phone, and he heard a buzzer in an office down the corridor.

'Reception, Docteur. Monsieur Dartson est ici.'

She smiled a pitifully brave smile and Doctor Foche in white coat appeared, solemn, a professional softness set in the line of his mouth.

'Monsieur Dartson.' A firm handshake, then the same hand on the shoulder.

'Eh bien voila . . . '

The explanation was hardly important.

Sarah had died in childbirth, the baby was a girl, very healthy considering, though in an oxygen tent at the moment.

He did not see any problems for her.

Sarah was dead.

Her child was alive, a baby girl.

As predicted.

3

Melanie again brought him breakfast.

She had tied her hair in a bun and wore a severe dress, grey, short sleeves, white belt. He could have been in hospital himself.

She drew back the curtains efficiently and when his eyes had become accustomed to the light he saw a clean white envelope next to the coffee cup.

'It's eleven o'clock. I thought it best to wake you.'

He took the envelope and saw Sarah's simple writing.

It was addressed to 'Daddy.'

He looked up and saw Melanie watching him, waiting for a reaction.

The reaction was deep inside, just above the stomach and coming up to the throat.

'She asked me to give it to you, the following morning.'

Melanie left, closing the door quietly.

He tore open the envelope and took out the small piece of writing paper.

My Darling Daddy,
Now that it has happened, as I knew it would, perhaps you will believe that there were powers working within me which are at present beyond your comprehension. It is so important for you to understand what I was capable of, and what you are capable of, that I beg you to allow Melanie to guide you through the maze of corridors beyond the door which I have unlocked for you. I know that this will mean a struggle, that you will try to reject the unbelievable, but in memory of me, please try. The hereafter is still a mystery and I do not claim to know about the dead.

I would like my daughter to be christened Emma and I would like to be buried next to Mummy.

Your loving daughter, Sarah.

He got up, washed and shaved slowly in the peace and privacy of his bathroom.

The wishes of the dead. He couldn't avoid them.

Melanie would of course know the contents of the letter, she might well have helped write it.

It was emotional blackmail.

He took her to the clinic to see the child, an experience which brought home the reality of the events of the recent past.

The curled-up baby, grey rather than pink, wired for life to various instruments and bottles, lay panting in the incubator, a numbered label tied round its tiny ankle.

Melanie gazed at it for a very long time, wide-eyed, like a child herself at a Christmas shop window, a meaningful motherhood feeling stirring within, no doubt.

He would have to stop being cynical about her, but it was his only means of defence.

Too much had happened, he was numb, he had lost those he loved, he was left with a small human being who would need love, he was alone, yet not alone at all. He was thankful Melanie was there, a buffer against all the unnecessary obligations that were crowding in on him.

* * *

She got him through the second funeral. David's parents dutifully came down, talked of the little girl, the grand-daughter they shared, talked of Sarah's possessions, what should be done, what should not be done, asking advice about investing the money Sarah and David had left to pay for the child's education. None of it mattered to him, not yet. He wanted time to recover, he needed time to breathe, to get back his bearings. The emptiness he felt was something he had never experienced, it drained him of any desire, nothing was worth living for, even the beauties of nature, the sunrises, the sunsets, the crystal-clear sea against the red Côte d'Azur rocks stirred nothing within him for a long time.

David's parents left after a week, after a lunch one day, a tea another, drinks another. Melanie coped with it all admirably, somehow getting the daily who came in to do the heavier housework to understand what was wanted and when.

He took tranquillizers to sleep, drank a good deal, went for walks alone up the hill past Renoir's old studio, seeing nothing, talking to no one.

Then one evening Melanie came up to the penthouse living room where he was sitting in the dark looking out across the fairy lights of the town.

'If I played you a recording of Sarah's voice, would it upset you?'

'Probably,' he said.

'It's important to me. Your reaction to what she says is important to me.'

He shrugged his shoulders.

She switched on a light and sat down next to him, a portable cassette recorder on her knees.

'It's a dream she had,' she said, and pressed the 'play' button.

There were several seconds of silence, a slight hum, then unexpectedly Sarah's voice came booming out, very loud. He thought Melanie would turn down the volume, but she didn't.

'I don't recall how I came up to the

door . . . ' the voice started, 'but it was a glass panelled door painted over in white, badly painted, with dust caught in the little strokes made by the brush. The door was ajar and I pushed it open. I was alone, my eyes level with the door knob so I must have been a small child . . . It was a bathroom, tiled. I'll come back to the tiles. In the bath was this woman with no hair. She looked terribly old. Terribly old. Her eyes were mauve all around and her breasts sagged like flat pouches of skin. She screamed when I saw her . . . when she saw me . . . and reached for a bundle of grey hair which must have been a wig. I quickly closed the door and ran down the corridor.'

There was a pause, then Melanie's voice said, 'Go on.'

'I remember a large green pot half-way down the corridor which I knocked over . . . I was very frightened, as frightened of having come upon the bald woman as I was of having knocked over the green pot. The strongest impression I got was of those bathroom tiles, an old bathroom it was with an old copper geyser. The

41

bathroom floor was made up of small diamond-shaped tiles in green, blue and white and they were familiar, they were friends, and I know that what made them friends was that they were in an irregular pattern which fascinated me. As a whole they gave the impression of a worked-out floor, but in fact two, or sometimes three greens might be together, then two blues together, sometimes not . . . '

There was another pause, a long one, then the voice went on.

'You know those mosaic games, wooden or plastic, which one had as a child, I think I had worked out how that floor should have been laid, and I went to that bathroom to play a mental game with the tiles . . . The woman was a relation.'

'Do you know who you were?' Melanie's voice asked.

'I think I must have been my father.'

'Has anyone spoken to you about seeing a bald woman in a bath?'

'I can't be sure. This is the area we fall into each time, isn't it? Is this dream imagined from a story one has heard, or is it inherited memory?'

And Melanie switched off the tape.

His mouth had gone dry.

'Please don't fight it,' Melanie said. 'It's too important. Sarah begged me to play it to you as soon as I could. I don't know if you remember but one lunchtime you mentioned your grandmother having a wig. She felt sure it was her in the dream. Was it? Does that scene mean anything to you at all?'

He sat up, leaned forward, took his time, chose his words carefully.

'Yes it does. It's a memory I have of my childhood, but it wasn't my grandmother, it was my grandmother's sister. My great-aunt, I suppose.'

He breathed out slowly.

'The tiles weren't green,' he went on. 'They weren't green or blue but very regular black and white squares.'

'So that was wrong.' Melanie looked concerned.

He could leave it at that. He could say nothing more, sympathize with her disappointment and bury the truth for ever. But what he had heard was so incredible, and it linked him so closely to Sarah, that he couldn't keep it to himself.

'The tiles were black and white and regular, they were in my great-aunt's bathroom in her Brooklyn apartment, and I used to go into that bathroom whenever the family visited her, to play a kind of game. I desperately wanted those tiles to be green and blue . . . and diamond shaped. Downstairs I've got a book I had as a child in which there is a picture of a Pierrot wearing a costume of green, blue and white diamonds. I wanted the bathroom floor to be like that. Don't ask me why . . . a childish fancy . . . I used to sit on the lavatory and imagine how I would change the floor. I saw my great-aunt in the bath on the day of my grandmother's funeral. She was getting ready to accompany my parents. It was the day I knocked over the pot of green plants.'

'Did you ever mention this to Sarah, or anyone else?'

'No. It was a totally private memory.'

'Yes,' Melanie said smiling. 'They're the ones I'm after.'

44

★ ★ ★

Doctor Foche came round the next day to give him a check-up and talk about Emma. Obviously they couldn't keep her at the clinic for ever and within a week she would be strong enough to come home. Michael therefore had to make a decision as to what would happen to her.

There were two alternatives, to send her to live with David's parents in England, or to look after her himself. He didn't want to lose her, she was a link with Sarah, with Norma, the problem was who would actually take care of her.

Doctor Foche suggested Melanie, and when he approached her on the subject it seemed that she had taken it for granted that she would become the child's nanny.

'I used to look after babies. I'm a trained children's nurse,' she said. 'The feeds are complicated, you know, and you have to get up in the middle of the night and change the nappies. Emma could have the room next to mine, that way you wouldn't be disturbed. But I wouldn't do it for nothing.'

45

'I don't know how much nannies get,' Michael said.

'With board it wouldn't be much. The only thing is I'll have to give up my bedsitter in London and go and collect my things, so I'd obviously like to know that it's for at least six months.'

He wrote her a letter confirming employment for a period of not less than six months, gave her a generous sum of money and suggested she should fly to London and collect all her possessions as soon as possible so that she could be back in a week to start her duties.

Efficient as ever, Melanie booked herself a flight the following morning and for the next few days Michael found himself alone again.

On the Thursday, after a snack lunch he drove to the clinic to see Emma. She had grown and had more colour, looked a little more human. She was out of the incubator and in a small cot in a room by herself. Tied to a corner of the cot was a label — Emma Dartson. They had given her his surname, presumably because he was footing the bill, or Sarah hadn't given her married name. For some reason she had always been proud of being a Dartson.

He turned the label over to see if there was anything on the reverse, the baby's weights and measures, but there was nothing, just the name printed through, ƎMMAᗡAᴚTꙄOͶ.

He stared at it.

NOSTRADAMME.

A posthumous joke?

* * *

When he got back to the villa the elevator engineers' van was parked outside and he remembered that it was the day of the quarterly visit when they checked that all was well.

He stopped the car behind the van expecting to find the two men waiting inside the gates in the drive, but he couldn't see them. Then he noticed the kitchen door was open, which was strange unless the daily woman had come back in the afternoon for something.

He went into the kitchen but found no

47

sign of her, so he went through to the drawing room and to the hallway; the elevator was ascending and one of the men was standing by the gates.

He asked who had let them in.

A young lady, the man explained, with reddish hair.

Melanie?

She had arrived unexpectedly then.

He went up the stairs, deliberately slowly. He was annoyed, but had to make sure not to show it. He wanted more time to think things out.

But in her room there was no evidence of her having arrived, no suitcases, no coat, nothing.

He started looking round the house — the small room which would be Emma's, next to the one Sarah and Melanie had shared, the third-floor bathroom, the box room and out onto the small terrace balcony.

The third floor with the guest suite, the guest sitting room, the double bedroom, the balcony. Up on the fourth floor, the penthouse sitting room — no sign of her, all as neat and tidy as he had left it.

He went down to the first floor, to his bedroom, where he found Sarah's dressing gown on his bed; it couldn't possibly have been there when he left. He picked it up; there was a smell about it which instantly reminded him of Melanie, a soap scent, not perfume. He went into the bathroom.

'Melanie?'

No one.

What the hell was happening?

He went quickly downstairs to the two men who were filling in their time-sheets for him to sign.

He questioned them again. How was the girl dressed? What did she look like? Did she speak with an accent? The answer was the same from both. Melanie in Sarah's dressing gown.

He signed their time sheets, saw them out of the gate, and looked all over the house again.

He could find nothing else unusual except his own bathroom window open. It wasn't open when he had left. He went out into the garden and the garage, calling her name out several times.

Nothing.

No one.

He couldn't make it out.

And when he sat down in the kitchen waiting for the kettle to boil to make himself a cup of coffee he realized that he was frightened.

Was it a premonition?

Had Melanie had an accident too?

Or was it Sarah coming back from the grave, placing her dressing gown in his room as a sign?

God!

Melanie had given him a number to ring in London in case he needed her. Well, he needed her. He needed an explanation, or at least he needed to know she was there, alive and well.

He turned off the kettle and went to the study; he picked up the phone and dialled.

She answered.

'Hallo?' Her timid voice was cautious at the other end.

'It's Michael. Just thought I'd ring to let you know Emma is quite strong now and can come out whenever we want.'

'Oh, good. I've explained the situation to my landlord here and he doesn't mind me leaving. He's already got someone else to take the room in fact, so I'll be coming on Sunday as arranged.'

'Look forward to seeing you,' he said.

A tense, nervous conversation, on both their parts. It was only when Michael put down the receiver that he remembered why he had rung Melanie in the first place. Well, she was alive, and certainly couldn't have flown down and back again in that short time.

He went upstairs and picked up Sarah's dressing gown.

Could he have had a lapse of memory, or sleep walked, or brought the gown down himself? But then the two men had seen a girl, talked to her, she had opened the door and let them in.

As evening fell he tried not to think about it; he watered the plants, rearranged his books, tidied quite a few papers. Eventually he went up to bed and, knowing he wouldn't sleep, took a Valium.

It did little for him. He just lay there

51

staring at the ceiling still wondering how Sarah's dressing gown could possibly have got from her cupboard to his bed, and how the men could have imagined Melanie. Then it occurred to him that maybe, a long shot, but maybe the daily's daughter, a fourteen year old who had come in once or twice to help her, might have come up to the house knowing where the key was hidden, perhaps put on Sarah's dressing gown, as children do, and had been surprised by the men, so let them in, and vanished. It would account for the bathroom window being open, the bell ringing, and her looking out to see who it was.

It made enough sense to be a consoling thought; it was a plausible explanation, and he decided that that was what had happened; he switched off the light and instantly entered a dream world he had previously visited, a hot, dank, sunbaked world of dust and intense pain and fear. Across the back of his neck was a yoke, on either side rope baskets weighed down by rocks. Bare feet, cruel stones he was trying to avoid, and up on the left, chained to the wall they were building, the bearded bony man with his long penis hanging between his skinny legs, and the small woman with the knife, now a quick upward gesture, the blade flashing momentarily in the sun, that cry of agony and the woman holding it up, dripping blood and throwing it into her companion's basket as though it were so much offal from a butcher, walking on past him to the next man chained on the wall. A glance backwards to see the man's expression, avoiding a glance down, unable not to. The blood, oh God the blood . . . then, suddenly, the impact of the closed fist in his back, stumbling, falling, one of the baskets of stones crushing his right hand, the huge negro picking him up. It'll be all right, they wouldn't do it to him, they wouldn't do it because he was far too good a worker. Then another guard, an Arab, armour-plated, leather, and iron chains, picking him up bodily and carrying him to the circle of grimacing women. The fat girl in the middle pinned down by the black matrons, her legs held apart; now himself,

53

still held, being fondled, excited, a lash across the back, laughter as he felt himself erecting despite the fear.

A stud, a white stud, valuable to the community as a white slave. Now the warmth, the moment of fondness, a woman astride his back jumping up and down, forcing him in, the fat girl moving, not struggling, grinning, enjoying the hideous copulation.

Then his ejaculation.

Now he saw this gaunt man being pulled from him, but he was the girl on the ground, watching the man he had been, hating him, looking at his own fear. He was being hauled up the wall, chained, there was pity for him and laughter. It was the injustice. Copulation with a Berber was punishable by death, by castration. He had been forced to do it, but he would have to pay. His feelings were mixed, his, hers, he was both, but he saw the scene through her eyes, and there was the small woman grabbing his testicles, squeezing them and the knife again and the sight of his genitals flying in the air like a bird, across the blue sky and landing in the basket with a flat, sick, wet noise, and then the frenzy and excitement as he was dismembered and his entrails dripped onto the sand and the knowledge that the dead man was him, seen through the woman whom he had also been.

*   *   *

Melanie duly arrived on the Sunday midday flight from London, and after driving her home to show her the pram he had bought and how he had changed the baby's room round and equipped it with cot, baby bath and play-pen, they went to collect Emma from the clinic.

Melanie got down to her nanny's duties immediately, even putting on a pink and white check nurse's uniform which would certainly impress the locals if nothing else.

All went remarkably well for two weeks. Doctor Foche called to see how Emma was getting on. Melanie looked after the child so quietly that Michael was hardly aware of their existence and was able to sit in his study and write all the letters he had to write, and make all the necessary business contacts he had to make to feel that he wasn't wasting his life. He knew, however, that his enthusiasm to start up again had gone. In time, no doubt, he would regain it, when there was a need to make money, when Emma perhaps started showing signs of individuality which he could help develop, but for the moment he felt drained of energy and had nothing to spur him on.

One afternoon, while he was getting together some documents relating to a major investment project for an old client who had docked his luxury yacht at Cannes and to whom he had promised advice, a very agitated couple from next door turned up with a hysterical Emma screaming in her pram. They had found her abandoned in the Renoir Museum gardens opposite, bawling her head off. Though Melanie had been seen with her earlier in the olive grove where she usually went to read in the afternoon, she had seemingly disappeared.

He successfully made the child a bottle, fed her on his knee as he had seen Norma do once or twice in the distant past, changed her nappy and, having put her in her cot, went quickly up the road to investigate. He would not call the police as his neighbours suggested until he had searched the Renoir gardens himself, a decision he was thankful to have taken for, following a track that led to a secluded grove, he found Melanie's clothes. Her check dress, her panties, her shoes. Had they been scattered and torn he would have been concerned, but they were neatly folded and placed under a tree hidden from normal view.

As he looked through her clothes, he heard a gentle cough behind him and, turning, was actually shocked to see the demure Melanie, quite nude, covering her small breasts with one hand and her pubic hair with the other.

'I'm terribly sorry,' she said. 'I was sunbathing and fell asleep.'

He couldn't believe it. Melanie, shy, retiring Melanie, had been sunbathing in the nude. He handed her her clothes, and said he'd wait for her in front of the Renoir house. At least the old man's ghost would not mind his garden being used for nudity.

Within minutes she came tip-toeing through the grass, barefoot, carrying her shoes, apologetic.

'Is Emma all right?'

'A somewhat neurotic couple from next door brought her down. She was crying her head off.'

'I don't know how I didn't hear her. I'm dreadfully sorry.'

He too was surprised she hadn't heard Emma. In fact her disappearance and reappearance reminded him of the strange incident with the two elevator engineers.

'I have to confess to something,' she said, as they started back to the house. 'I took a sleeping pill last night, and I think it had a delayed effect.'

'I've put Emma to bed and changed her nappy, in reverse order,' he said. 'She seemed calm enough. Do babies suffer traumas for life if left alone too long?'

'No. It's good for them. If you obey their every cry they become spoilt.'

The discussion on how to bring up

babies got them to the house.

It was all very well trying to put other people's strange behaviour to the back of his mind, but it was not so easy. One thing which didn't fit comfortably into Melanie's story was the simple fact that she never sunbathed. Virtually the first thing he had learned about her when he had collected her and Sarah at the airport was that 'Melanie goes red and burns easily.' So why the sudden change now, in the middle of a hot afternoon without creams or sun-tan lotions? And why in public gardens and not on the roof terrace?

A man? Had she given herself to the Renoir Museum gardener, one of those lusty Algerians, and in her ecstasy totally forgotten Emma, indeed totally forgotten herself? Or had it been so good that she had promptly fallen asleep afterwards and the bastard had left her side to continue hoeing? Or decamped fast on hearing someone approach?

Whatever it was, she would certainly no longer be able to play the innocent.

He went back to his study and finished

getting the file together for his client in Cannes. He thought little more of Melanie, at least in the terms of her strange behaviour, but he did think of her as a great help. Without her he would certainly have had to hire a nurse, and finding one that was as quiet and hard working as her would have been difficult.

After putting away all his papers he went to the kitchen for a glass of water and saw a note on the table.

'Have gone shopping in the village with Emma.'

From now on she was obviously going to let him know where she was going, to reduce her guilt no doubt, though the evening walk to the shops was fairly routine. Maybe she met friends down there, maybe her Algerian lover, the gardener?

On the way up to the penthouse, without premeditation, he decided to peep into her room, to see how she had arranged things.

He pushed her bedroom door open and entered Melanie's neat, private little world.

The main surprise was the full-length mirror which she had taken from the

60

adjoining bathroom and hung lengthwise on the wall next to her bed, so that when lying down she could see herself full length.

On the chest of drawers two blue candles in white porcelain candlestick-holders flanked a large family photograph in a silver frame. Turn-of-the-century American farmers, the men in ill-fitting white collars and bowlers, the women in high-necked black dresses with sleeveless white overalls. The back-drop was the proverbial verandah of a wooden shack; there were no dogs, but three black cats. The faces gave nothing away except a determination to look intelligent and serious in front of the camera. None of them looked particularly like Melanie.

The book by her bedside table was an old leather-bound English-French version of *The Prophecies of Nostradamus*.

Nostradamus again!

It was ear-marked in several places and he read a quatrain circled in pencil.

Auprès d'oliviers et nudité étoile
Parent du vingt et unième, unique au

monde.
Divine, sa mère bientôt sous voile.
Père mort d'une chute étroite et profonde.

He glanced at the translation.

Near olive trees and nudity by starlight
Parent of the twenty first, unique on earth.
Divine, his mother soon under veil
Father dead of narrow and deep fall.

He didn't understand a word of it.

He closed the book, more puzzled than enlightened, eased open the top drawer of a chest of drawers that had been in his New York bedroom, and looked in. Neat, tidy, socks, stockings, tights, a T-shirt he had never seen her wear, various toiletries.

In the second drawer were her sweaters, neatly folded, smelling of moth balls. The third drawer was locked.

It was intriguing.

He had absolutely no right to know

what was in there, and she had absolutely every reason to keep some of her belongings a secret.

But he was curious.

Norma had always kept a box of odd keys as she had boxes of buttons, of ribbons, of corks, or assorted pins and he remembered having put it appropriately away in the boxroom.

Stealthily, a burglar in his own house, he went to get it, then came back up to the room. He examined the lock, a standard lock, and found several likely keys. The second one worked like magic, he eased the drawer open and found three rolls of white parchment paper, rolled up, and a black metal deeds box which was locked.

He took out one of the rolls and carefully laid it out on the bed as its sheer length forbade him to hold it up.

It was a family tree, written out in exemplary gothic script, a detailed chart of a family called GREGORIEV, related to Grigori Yefimovich Rasputin (1871–1916). The last entry was a certain Grigori Gregoriev, against whose name were bracketed the words: [Delegate United Nations].

The second roll, another family tree, was that of the CAPUELA family descended from the Sforzas with a line marked 'Unconfirmed' leading to the name Niccolo Machiavelli (1469–1527). The last but one entry was an Italian delegate to the European Economical Council.

So Melanie had at one time been doing researches for persons connected with international politics. That could be useful! And as he was tracing the Capuela line of ascendancy to the top of the chart, he became aware that someone had come into the room behind him.

Glancing at the reflection in the mirror, he saw Melanie standing in the doorway.

4

She was not angry. She was smiling, a smile that hinted at victory. If she had wished that one day his curiosity about her would get the better of him, then that wish had been granted.

'Who,' he asked in a loud clear voice, acknowledging her presence, 'are the Capuelas, and why all this work on them?'

He turned to face her.

'I used to do family trees, those are copies.'

He straightened up, pleased that he had momentarily managed to overcome his guilt.

'I'm sorry I intruded on your privacy like this, but I was looking for something which might have been left in the drawer during the move,' he lied, not very well.

She smiled at him again, and glanced at the key in the lock, then at the open box of keys on the bed.

'I did a thorough job,' he admitted.

'You're curious about what Sarah and I have been up to, and I think it's time you admitted it.'

He shrugged his shoulders.

'Allow me to show you more.'

She picked out the third roll, carefully took off the elastic band and spread it out on top of the others on the bed.

It was an even more detailed family tree and she pointed to a name at the bottom. His — Michael Dartson.

The name beneath it was Sarah's and pencilled in was 'Emma.' Also pencilled in was a line to a space reserved for the name of Emma's husband, and a line coming down from that union to a space for their offspring.

He scanned the various names of his supposed forefathers. Michael D'Artson, Immaculada Almargo, Emmanuelle La Notte, Michel Le Nostre, Marie Chapelet de Nostredamme . . . and then at the top MICHEL DE NOSTREDAMME (Nostradamus).

He looked at her amused. 'I'm descended from Nostradamus?

'I'm sorry, I get Nostradamus, Copernicus and Cagliostro mixed up. Weren't they all magicians?'

'Cagliostro was an eighteenth century Italian charlatan who claimed he could make gold and extend life by five thousand years. Copernicus was Polish, lived in the sixteenth century and was a serious and very respected astronomer. Nostradamus, who lived at the same time, was a Royal doctor and astrologer with amazing psychic precognitive powers who accurately foretold the future, not only for his contemporaries but for us as well. He had premonitions of both world wars, countless modern disasters and even John and Robert Kennedys' assassinations.'

'And he's one of my ancestors?'

She nodded.

'Is that why Sarah wanted Emma called Emma, because it spelt his name backwards?'

'Yes. If you look at the chart you'll see the name has never been lost for long, there has always been someone who knew of the connection.'

He studied the chart. 'You've got my great-grandmother, Sarah Field, down as the daughter of a man called René Marcel; she was the daughter of Captain John Field, famed for his part in the Battle of Balaclava, the only family hero we've got!' he said.

She lifted the deeds box from the drawer and opened it with a key she had in her pocket. It was packed tight with papers, letters, documents.

'All this is research on your family.' She handed him a bundle of papers to hold, and he glanced at the typed transcript on top.

On the 25th Frimaire of the year (41796) Citizen François Hugon, carpenter by profession, residing in Limoges, Rue des Colombier, Section de l'Egalité, being of legal age, was united to Citizen Emmanuelle Le Notre, a minor and legitimate daughter of Jacques Lenotre and Jeanne Poiret. The chief witness was a friend, the other three witnesses were relatives of the bride.

He looked at the page underneath.

In the year of grace 1784, on the 9th January, a new-born child, a foundling boy, was baptized by me. He was given the name Jaume. (In accordance with custom the abandoned child without identification papers receives only a Christian name.)

Signed: Abbé Leblanc.

Stapled to this document was another.

Confession: 1799. April 3.
Citizen Emmanuelle Hugon confessed to being the mother of the foundling boy Jaume Lanotte, born in great sin, the father being her own father Jacques Le Notre, deceased a month ago. May his soul rest in peace.

It was extraordinary.

He looked at the sheer volume of work all her researches had entailed and it was mind-boggling. The cross-references alone, the dating of every document, the writing out of the chart which, in its own way, was a work of art. He couldn't understand how just one person could have done it all.

'This must have taken you years.'

'I have a trick or two up my sleeve to help me get the right source quickly.'

He glanced at the chart again. The sheer history of it!

Jacob Le Nostre (1682–1734), union with Fatima Ouled Hariz, their son Michel Le Nostre born in Meknes, mercenary killed during the battle of Rossbach fighting for Prussians under Frederick II.

'What happened here? Between Emmanuelle La Notte and Immaculada Almargo?' he asked, pointing to a blank space.

'That's one of the areas I still have to check, that and the connection between Jeanne Chapelet and Marie Chapelet de Nostredamme.'

He was impressed.

'I know that Emmanuelle La Notte came from a village called St Aubin les Bois, near Digne, so I'll have to go there, check through the local church records, if any, and then the council records. As for the Chapelet connection, it's a matter of going to all sorts of places and doing some research.'

'Digne isn't very far. We could go there and back in a day,' he said, smiling at her. 'Were you counting on me suggesting that?'

'Eventually.'

'Well, it's my family history, so it's only natural that I should be enthusiastic. It's all that supernatural rubbish I was keeping at arm's length.'

'But this is all part of the supernatural rubbish as you call it.'

'Because of the Nostradamus connection?' he asked, amused.

'Not only because of that, but because of the predictory powers it has given you.'

'I've never predicted anything in my life.'

'No? Think about it while I go and get Emma's bottle ready. Think about how you came to be so rich so easily, for instance.'

She left him looking at the chart of his family tree.

He heard her go downstairs, but didn't move; he stayed staring first at the chart then out of the window at the tops of the trees.

Over the years, despite all doubts and uncertainties gripping investors, business men and economists, he had predicted a correct growth in production, incomes and profits of four major corporations which had been in the red, and had foreseen two spectacular bankruptcies before anyone suspected such financial disasters. The clients that had trusted him had prospered; he had no idea what had happened to the many who had ignored his advice.

Was Melanie suggesting then that his business acumen, his nose for a good investment was due to predictive powers? It was because he studied the markets and kept himself well informed. Admittedly the National Systems Bank affair had been strange, a seemingly mad gamble he'd taken which had paid off handsomely when a cash-laden Saudi Arabian had stepped in out of the blue. What had made him buy those shares?

Not a vision, not a premonition, but the names of the people and companies involved had inexplicably come to him.

Like the paintings he'd bought.

He'd made quite a bit speculating in modern art as a hobby. In fact he'd developed quite a flair for spotting the work of artists before they became fashionable.

Raulk, for one.

When Melanie came up with Emma, fed and ready for bed, he was still standing over the chart looking at all the names, the dates, the notes.

'You don't actually have any proof of a Nostradamus connection, do you?' he said. 'It's all supposition.'

'Supposition based on Sarah's dreams which have had extraordinary results.'

'What sort of dreams?'

'Well, for instance, she was able to describe a particular building in a certain town which she saw in her dreams so clearly that we were able to trace it, though she had never been there in her life.'

'What town was that?'

'Weymouth. Your great-great-grandmother, Mariana Fainhope, went there for a brief holiday. My theory is that memory is inherited, like features, so that you, as Sarah's father, one generation nearer to the past, should be able to recall totally what she could only recall partially. For example, can you remember a dream you had, a day-dream maybe, like a vision, a 'memory', where a building is involved? You're there in front of it and to you it is awesome, a little frightening, and demands your attention?'

'Does it have to be a tall building? An old one?'

'It has to be what you recall as awesome, a place which you feel you may never leave once you've entered it.'

'Like a prison?'

'Maybe. But this isn't a guessing game,' she said smiling. 'Just think of a building that made an impression on you, though you may never have been there.'

He closed his eyes to please her and, for no apparent reason, a picture flashed across his mind of a low grey building, not that old, in a tree-lined avenue, plane

74

trees, probably France, two storeys, a long wall, with very few windows, but a large gate. Barracks? He hesitated.

'Say whatever comes into your head, quickly. The secret is not to analyse, not to think,' Melanie urged. 'You must not be inhibited about your thoughts. No one is going to laugh.'

'Well, what came into my mind, for what it's worth, just now, was a long low building, rather like barracks, in France. I think it's in France because of the tree-lined avenue. Plane trees.'

'What time of year?'

'Summer. The shadows of the leaves play on the walls.'

'How do you get in?'

'Big entrance gate, huge doors, portals, painted green. There's a courtyard beyond.'

'Anyone around?'

'People in white. There's a nurse. It could be a hospital.'

Trying to hold back a smile, Melanie got up and opened a drawer of the bedside table, brought out the cassette recorder and clipped in a cassette she took from another drawer full of tapes.

She pressed the 'play' button and Sarah's voice spoke out, sounding much younger than on the last recording he had heard.

'It's a long grey wall with small windows and right in the middle there is a large gate with green doors, an opening with huge green doors, and there's a soldier standing there wearing a blue uniform with a red stripe down the side of his trousers.' She paused, then went on, 'There are trees, many trees and a nurse with a long skirt and pointed black shoes. There's a man with a bowler hat, rather Edwardian — rather Lautrecish. I have a feeling of Toulouse-Lautrec, maybe because the man in the bowler hat is small and has a walking stick, but it's more than that, it's a feeling of his freedom as against my . . . I feel my time is limited . . . I feel my time is limited due to illness.'

That was absolutely what he'd felt. Lautrec and the feeling of limited time.

'Could be France,' Sarah's voice went on, 'Outskirts of Paris . . . but it's too provincial.'

Melanie stopped the tape.

'Now,' she asked, 'looking down the road, what did you see?'

He was still there outside the long low building. He looked down the road, could remember it quite clearly.

'An avenue leading to a square,' he said. 'The road's cobbled, there's the French flag on a building, and a church.'

'There's a shop somewhere. Can you see the name?'

'Yes. Carbien, the saddle maker.' And he stopped. How did he know this? He couldn't actually see it, but he could sense it.

'Fantastic!' Melanie said with girlish enthusiasm, and from the deeds box she brought out a postcard.

What he had described was there in sepia. The church, the shop, the long low building. It was an old postcard of the Toulon Military Hospital. He'd never heard of it in his life.

'Your great-great-grandfather died in that hospital, and he knew he would before he went in. You inherited his death anxieties,' Melanie said.

'Oh come on! My great-great-grandfather died in Yorkshire, Captain John Field of the Crimea.' Such misinformation was going to make him lose respect for the accuracy of her charts.

'The man who died in Yorkshire and which all your family were led to believe was your great-great-grandfather was not your great-great-grandfather by blood. He was your great-great-grandmother's husband, a quite different thing.'

'Are you suggesting illegitimacy?'

'I am suggesting exactly that. In your family tree this has occurred not once, but five times, possibly six. It does in most family trees.'

'So, according to you, I'm not related to John Field?'

'Only by marriage.'

'What proof have you got?'

Yet again she went to the deeds box and brought out a pile of documents.

'These are copies of the various birth, marriage and death certificates relating to the Field and Marcel families.' She explained: 'You will see that Mariana Fainhope-Field gave birth to Sarah Field on the 22nd July 1855 in Northallerton, Yorkshire, but that during the ten months that preceded her birth John Field was in the Crimea, indeed at the battle of Balaclava on the 25th October 1854. Sarah, therefore, could not have been his daughter. Her true father was in fact René Marcel, a French sailor from Toulon who happened to be staying in Weymouth in October 1854 when Mariana was there on holiday. I have a letter from René Marcel recalling their meeting to prove it. And this,' she said handing him a faded document, 'is Mariana Fainhope's marriage certificate to Captain John Field, dated 2nd June 1855, only two months before Sarah was born.'

'Why did he marry her?'

'They were engaged before he left for the Crimea and if the truth had been known at the time it would have disgraced the family. As it is Mariana must have been looked down on, as she was Spanish.'

'So my great-great-grandfather was French?'

'A French sailor. Can you imagine the

horror of it, only forty years after Waterloo? The Fields must have been ready to pay anyone to cover up such a scandal.'

Michael looked at the chart again. Great-great-grandmother Mariana conceived with French sailor, result his great-grandmother Sarah who conceived with a mad Irishman resulting in his crazy but lovable grandfather Michael d'Artson.

'How the hell did you unearth all that?'

'Mostly research.'

'But to go from a Yorkshire estate to Toulon . . .'

'Letters explain everything, when they exist.'

She handed him a letter from the Crimea dated 2nd November, 1854, mentioning the famous battle.

'Can't you imagine it? Young Mariana bored in Weymouth, her future husband thousands of miles away on the battlefield, meets up with this dashing young Frenchman, she possibly spoke French, their Mediterranean blood bubbles up . . .'

'*I* can imagine it. I didn't think your mind ran to such things.'

'My mind runs to everything.'

The look she gave him was surprisingly brazen, suddenly making him aware that he was in her bedroom.

'Any more skeletons in the cupboard?'

'Several. But as they go farther back into the past they become less interesting. Morals weren't so prim, sex was not so immoral.'

'What did he die of, this noble sailor from Toulon?'

'The noble sailor from Toulon died of syphilis.'

'You have a record of that, I suppose?'

And unbelievably she pulled out his death certificate from the deeds box.

'Is it inherited along with memory?' he asked, smiling.

'Physical diseases can be cured by medicine,' she said, putting all the papers away. 'Anxieties are something else.'

'What anxieties did Sarah inherit from me?'

'I don't know. Maybe all the fearfulness in your life is yet to come, and you'll pass the traces onto your son.'

'What son?' he asked, amazed.

'You're still young. Maybe you'll have a son.'

It was not such an outrageous idea, he had quite often thought of having a son, but with Norma . . .

'How can you say things like that?' he objected, however. He did not want to be dragged into admitting that he remotely believed everything she was suggesting. 'How can you even draw up this chart and make me a descendant of . . . one of the great names in history!'

'Study the family tree and you'll see that it's all very plausible. You're not only a descendant of Nostradamus, but you have inherited his powers of clairvoyance.'

'How do you know?'

'It runs in your family.'

'My parents weren't clairvoyant.'

'Are you sure?'

'Well, it was never mentioned.'

'They might not have known. Most people have no idea what they're capable of. We have hundreds of thoughts daily, we imagine a great deal, and if those

82

imaginings are separated and analysed and placed in the right pigeon-holes, they often add up to something. We have memory banks, not only our own but our parents' and grandparents' and forefathers'. 'Déjà vu' for instance can be a foresight but can also be a memory handed down. A colour, a smell that makes one feel either good or fearful, may not be related to one of our own experiences but to something experienced by one of our parents, or distant forbears. What's your favorite colour?' she asked suddenly.

'I don't know.'

'Of course you know. It's not a banal question, it's simple little things like that which add up to a total awareness of oneself. What is your favourite colour?' She asked again.

'I suppose . . . It depends for what, surely. For a room, a car, a toothbrush, a tie?'

'If you had to live for a year in a room . . . '

'Blue, because it's relaxing.'

'To you it's relaxing, to others it's cold.

My colour is a certain shade of green, a grass green. I never knew why till I went to visit my folks' place in Virginia. When the car turned the corner into the valley where my grandparents lived I was instantly struck by the feeling of being at home. I knew the colours, the shades and one particular shade which covered the whole of the hillside opposite their house. But I'd never been there before.'

'Maybe I like blue because I stared up at the sky from my pram?' he said unkindly.

The determined, patient look she gave him made him wish he hadn't said it.

'You're a very special person,' she said, 'and if you worked on yourself you could also become very powerful.'

5

'You're still young, maybe you'll have a son. You're a very special person, you could also become very powerful.'

It had been said simply, as a fact.

Over dinner he asked Melanie, 'What about this trip to Digne, to St Aubin les Bois for your researches?'

'Would you want to go?'

'Why not?'

'What would we do with Emma?'

'We could take her with us. She can lie in her carry-cot in the back.'

'And we could have a picnic!'

'No. One of the main attractions of travelling for me is eating in restaurants, specially in France.'

'Why aren't you fat?' she asked.

'I am. I just hide it very well.'

She smiled, an intimacy was growing between them.

'All we do tomorrow morning,' he said, 'is leave the house, lock the door and get into the car. It isn't a major expedition, and if we are delayed we'll stay the night in a hotel.'

'I'd best take Emma's feeds for twenty-four hours then.'

They ate in silence for a while. Then Melanie collected the empty plates, took them to the kitchen and returned with the fruit.

'I'd like to ask you about a certain stream of memory you may have had. It concerns the researches I want to do in St Aubin, and could save us a good deal of time.'

'Of course. What do I have to do?'

'Just relax and talk.'

'Can we go up to the penthouse?'

'Yes, ideal.'

They went up in the elevator, stopping on the second floor for Melanie to collect the cassette recorder and the deeds box.

'How many dreams do you have which recur?' she asked, when he had settled in the corner of the sofa with a brandy.

'Two, three . . . '

'Is it two or three?'

'Three' he said.

'What are they about, briefly?'

He breathed out, still reluctant to get involved, but he didn't have to think, he knew them so well, had had them too often, might get relief in fact by talking about them.

'One's about cannibalism, quite horrible. I get fearful hunger pains, it always takes place under medieval arches, in a vault of some kind; there are hundreds of people, poor, in rags, all hungry, and I see a naked baby which I believe to be dead, opening its eyes in terror as it is dropped in a boiling cauldron. I have a terrible feeling of guilt at what I'm allowing to happen, then the child's leg, white, wet, jelly-like, is proffered. It's hideous.'

He looked up, Melanie was listening intently, sitting crosslegged and sipping a glass of tonic water. She could have been a guru psychiatrist.

'Another concerns a man being emasculated. The third, I suppose, takes place during the 1914 war. I get buried by a mound of earth in the trenches.'

'You mustn't be surprised by what I tell you,' Melanie said after a moment. 'I don't expect you to believe me at first either, but eventually you will see that my theory of inherited memory is quite extraordinary. The three dreams you just mentioned are among the recurring ones Sarah had, and they are not dreams, but memories handed down to you.' She spoke with authority, she was making a statement, not trying to impress.

'The cannibalism one, which was her strongest, was possibly an occurrence experienced in a siege. The castration, which is followed by forced intercourse between a young Arab girl and a man is unusual, because it is inherited from both mother and father; we've dated that back to the eighteenth century, the time of the despot Moulay Ismail, who built the town of Meknes in Morocco.'

She was like a magician bringing surprises out of a hat.

'The buried-under-mud memory is the one I'm most interested in. I haven't been able to date it.' She leaned over and switched on the cassette recorder, adjusted it so that the microphone on the table faced him. The very sight of the instrument put him off, he disliked the sound of his own voice and talking into a microphone about his personal dreams was even more inhibiting.

He cleared his throat, decided to light a cigarette and did so, aware that the tape was going round. Melanie was patient, seemingly knowing what he was going through, aware that he wouldn't start immediately.

He took a puff, sent some smoke billowing towards the recorder, watched it being enveloped by the grey mist, wondered whether smoke spoiled the sound, then cleared his throat again.

He closed his eyes and tried to recall the dream. He then opened his eyes and looked at her.

'Do you want this in the present tense or the past?'

'It doesn't matter at all. Try it in the present, as though you were reliving it.'

'I'll start with the moment of fearfulness and maybe work backwards. Ask questions, I think it helps . . . The fearfulness then, the end . . . follows a muffled explosion, not loud, like a bomb going off underground, but a vast, overwhelming cloak of mud rises out of the ground and falls on me. It is heavy and wet and for a moment I struggle, aware of the taste in my mouth which is, quite simply, that of earth. It's not a terrible taste, but one which I have learned is not safe . . . poisonous . . . so I try to spit it out, but as I part my lips to do so . . . more earth comes in and I realize, all this in a fraction of a second, that I am going to suffocate. To test this I breathe in through my nostrils and more earth comes up right into the back of my throat, through my nose, and I start to choke, but I cannot choke because the mud has completely enveloped me. Then I realize that this is the end. This is how it is going to be. I am being buried alive, a shell has exploded near me, I have not been blown to bits, my body will remain intact, but I will be buried alive. I think this is stupid, I am at the same time thankful that I am not mutilated and incredulous that this is it, this is how it is going to end, after so many years of speculation, that it might be the sword or

90

the bayonet, this is how it is going to be . . . and then I am paralysed by the thought of taking my next breath for I will be unable to, and I have the knowledge that I have already taken my last breath. I try to breathe in, need to, cannot, swallow mud, I then blow . . . and this has some effect. I breathe in through my mouth, aware that I am breathing in my own air. I blow out again, feel my hands moving, struggling as though they are pinned to my side, but I can move them and I get my left hand up to my mouth and clear away the mud, I open my eyes and see daylight, I realize the end isn't to be quite yet. I have survived again, I spit out the mud, blow my nose . . . I choke now . . . there is pain in my lungs, but I can breathe. That is what is painful. Living is painful, the breath of life is painful . . . '

He stopped to stub out his unsmoked cigarette. He could feel the pain in his lungs, as he had felt it several times before.

'What do you see now?' Melanie asked.

He kept his eyes closed, was totally relaxed, sitting well back, enjoying the sound of her analytical question.

'The wheel of a cannon.'

'Are you above it or below it?'

'I'm looking up at it. I'm lying on the ground, under it. I'm under it and the cannon is in fact upside down. It's a 12-pounder Gribeauval . . . ' he heard himself say.

He sat up and looked at Melanie.

'How on earth would I know that?'

'It's your cannon probably. You're in the artillery. But go on . . . what colour is your uniform?'

'Khaki.'

'Are you sure?'

He closed his eyes, saw his hand and his sleeve. The sleeve wasn't khaki, it was green. His jacket was green, covered with mud it looked khaki.

'It's green,' he said. 'I'm a sergeant in the artillery and we're fighting the Austrians.'

It all came out quite suddenly. He knew all this, he had a wealth of knowledge to pour out and he closed his eyes and prayed that Melanie would not interrupt.

'I'm twenty-five. I've enlisted in Napoleon's army, and we're fighting the Austrians near the Danube. We have been waiting for days to do battle. We are so strong, so well equipped that we know we will win. Our only fear is that we may not kill as many of the enemy as our rival platoon, and that is all that matters to me, that and wanting to please my commander, and be respected by my men. I have only just been promoted, but I am well esteemed. This is quite extraordinary,' he said, unable to believe what was in his mind. 'I am also terrified now that I have lost a leg. The whole of my right side is numb and I realize that my right hand feels sticky. I am looking at it and it is red with my own blood and I can't move . . . and now Pierrot . . . my friend Pierrot . . .'

Quite inexplicably he felt himself go very weak. He tried to open his eyes, but was overcome by nausea.

He eventually looked up to find himself staring at Melanie, who was wiping his brow with a damp towel from her bathroom and pressing a glass of water to his lips.

93

'You fainted. I expect your men were lifting the cannon off your leg, and the pain was too much.' She smiled. She wasn't laughing at him, she was very serious.

'But it's ridiculous,' he said, sitting up. He had never fainted in his life yet he could clearly remember the pain he had just experienced.

'You have incredible recall. Sarah had the same dream but she never got farther than struggling in the mud. We always thought the man had died then, but of course he couldn't have done so or the memory would not have been passed down. What we have to do now is fix that memory to a time and place and see if it makes sense.'

She left the room to go and get the chart.

He sat there aware that he had been perspiring, incredulous that he could relive something that had happened in the past.

He took a sip of water, put down the glass and wiped his face before she returned. He still didn't want to admit that he believed, and didn't want to appear to have suffered during the experience.

'Jaume Lanotte,' she said, coming back, 'lived during the Napoleonic wars. You mentioned Austrians and the Danube. Could it have been the battle of Wagram, in 1809?'

She sat down next to him and indicated the blank space on the chart. From it a line went to Immaculada Almargo and her daughter Mariana Fainhope, born in Malaga, 1829.

'How could you make that connection?'

'Working backwards from your great-grandparents. It's not a hundred percent certain, but the name Lanotte fits. If we can connect Lanotte with Immaculada Almargo, we're home and dry. If he was a soldier in Napoleon's army he might have gone to Spain. When was the battle of Salamanca?'

'1811, 1812?' he suggested. He wasn't sure.

'It could fit.'

★   ★   ★

From rough calculations on the map it looked like a three-hour drive to St Aubin les Bois. If they left by ten they could have a comfortable lunch there.

It was a bright sunny morning with dew still on some of the leaves, and Michael found having morning coffee and toast in the kitchen with Melanie, instead of alone in bed, extremely pleasant. She had got up earlier, fed Emma and placed her in the cot. He had come down in his dressing gown. They were a family. It was like Norma, himself and Sarah when he was younger, only somehow now he was so much more relaxed. He doubted that he was actually falling for Melanie, but certainly the idea of living with her on a more permanent basis was not so ridiculous.

They finished breakfast, he washed up his cup and plate and went up to get ready.

He had to admit that she had fired his enthusiasm. As he shaved, the electric buzz confirmed that he was still in this world, his reflection in the mirror that he still looked physically the same. Yet he had had these extraordinary recollections. They were in no way frightening. They were not particularly mysterious, it was certainly not ghostly. The 'recalls' were like reading an enthralling history book. But to be able to relive the lives of others was surely incredible? He wanted to try again.

★   ★   ★

Melanie carefully arranged the gurgling Emma in the back seat together with a briefcase full of essential documents and her cassette recorder.

They drove to Grasse, then stopped for coffee at Castellane.

'What exactly are we going to do when we get to St Aubin?' he asked.

'We make enquiries about the Lanotte family at the post office, the gendarmerie, the mairie. If we draw blanks there we go to the church and ask the priest for the marriage registers, hopefully he will be old and may remember families. Invariably one thing leads to another and one gets to someone who remembers someone who remembers a direct link.'

'Don't people think it strange that you should be making enquiries into their family past?'

'It all depends. With officials I always show proof that I am a professional researcher, a young girl can always get around stubborn old men, anyway. With others I tell them I'm writing a history book. Everyone likes the idea of having their name in print.'

'Shall we drive on?'

They got back into the warm car, checked that Emma was as fast asleep as she seemed, got to Digne and turned off onto a minor road.

At noon they reached St Aubin les Bois and Michael stopped under the trees in the main square so that Melanie could feed Emma, who was now awake and making demanding noises.

The inevitable game of *boules* was in progress, the youngsters of the village going home from school on their bikes with their sticks of bread, the workers from the local factories on mopeds. The smell in the air from every house promised a gourmet meal and made him hungry.

Melanie spotted a small cafe which was certainly not what he was looking for, so he got out of the car, crossed the road and asked a fat and prosperous-looking man where it would be recommended to eat.

'Chez Auguste, à la sortie de la ville.'

He drove there slowly, finding Chez Auguste a quite delightful little restaurant with terrace outside on the pavement enclosed by bushes under a red awning.

He could think of nothing better.

He parked the car so that they could be within earshot of Emma from the restaurant, and chose a corner table outside.

He ordered Bayonne ham and a local Provençal dish. Melanie, uncertain, asked him to choose for her, so he ordered the same with a bottle of local red wine.

As the waiter took the order Michael noticed her staring across the street with a certain amount of concern.

He followed her gaze to a row of shops, a charcuterie, an electrician's, a boutique, but couldn't see anything of interest.

'The name of that butcher's,' she said.

He looked. CHARCUTERIE LAN-OTTE.

'That's an extraordinary coincidence,' he said.

'I usually try to find another explanation.'

She then darted a look across the street again and suggested he should do the same. Going in by the side entrance was the very man he had asked about the restaurant.

'Coincidence?' she asked.

'He's the charcuterie's grandfather, that's all,' Michael said.

'I wonder why you happened to choose him, though?'

'He was fat and prosperous.'

Melanie very nearly spoiled the meal with her obvious impatience, but she made it so clear that she was trying desperately not to do just that, that Michael appreciated the effort. Twice, quite unnecessarily, she went over to the car to see if Emma was sleeping peacefully, and once she glanced at her watch.

'The shops open at two,' he said in answer to that gesture, and she apologised for being rude.

'Tell me about your family.'

'What do you want to know?' she asked.

'Everything. Brothers, sisters, father, mother.'

'I'm an orphan and an only child. My parents died in an air crash in 1965.'

He was about to ask whether that had been predicted, but thought better of it.

'My father was a farmer, it was his first flight. They were coming to see me in New York.'

'I'm sorry,' he said. It didn't quite go with the sipping of the pleasant wine and the munching of the delicious cheese. 'What were you doing in New York?'

'Working in the general reference section of the Mid-Manhattan library.'

'When did you go to England?'

'Shortly afterwards. I had to get away, and I got an opening through someone who worked at the American Embassy.'

He saw from the corner of his eye that the charcuterie across the road was opening. He said nothing, but quickly ordered a coffee and asked for the bill. She could not help a smile and glanced over her shoulder as the charcutier opened the door and came out with the long pole to push up the metal shutters.

'Do you want a coffee?' Michael asked.

'With milk.'

She'd eaten like a bird, picked at the ham and only toyed with the beef. Maybe she was a vegetarian.

'Do you not like meat?'

'Sometimes. I'm not over fond of it.'

'Fish?'

'I prefer fish to meat. I don't really like eating animals, it seems wrong.'

'You must think me an ogre then?'

'No. Everyone to his own taste. I guess I was never quite brought up to be a gourmet. Though Mum used to make delicious rabbit pies . . . '

It was the first time he had seen her wistful.

'You've never been married?' he asked. It was a lead-in to the next question, and he was surprised that it made her blush.

'No!'

'Boyfriends?'

'Not in your sense of the word.'

'What's my sense of the word?'

'Sleeping with a boy?'

And she got up, picked up her bag and indicated that she was going through to the ladies' room.

He paid the bill, got up and went over to the car to see if his granddaughter was still asleep.

The small head of furry gold hair was peeping over the blanket, eyes firmly closed, a look of complete peace on its little face.

He had no idea what his feelings were for the child. She didn't belong to him yet, she wouldn't till she smiled at him and recognized him. She didn't particularly remind him of Sarah, more of his own father. For the moment, anyway, she was Melanie's child. It was all to do with who was responsible for feeding her and changing the nappies.

Melanie joined him and looked through the window.

'She's all right. She'll sleep through till about four.'

He took her by the arm, crossed the road and led her to the charcuterie. It was like taking a schoolgirl to a cosmetic shop, she seemed so excited.

'Can you do the talking, my French isn't too good?' she said.

'What do you want me to ask?'

'How long they've been living here and how old is the oldest member of the family.'

'Lanotte is probably a local name you know, there may be hundreds of them around.'

'Let's just try anyway.'

A young man with a moustache, and wearing a butcher's apron over a white coat was sharpening a knife in the fresh meat area of the shop. Behind the charcuterie counter was a woman who could have been his mother.

Michael went through a rather uncertain preamble about interpreting for Melanie who was a researcher in family trees and who was trying to trace a family connection to the beginning of the century. He wondered whether there were any old members of her family in the

104

village, or nearby who could help?

The woman behind the counter clapped her hands in wonderment. Her husband's mother, her mother-in-law, would be fascinated; she had been collecting everything about the family for years and only last night had gone on and on about how much a certain history book would cost. She was always reading books. Her father had been a teacher of course, which is where she had got it from.

He translated all this for Melanie who smiled at the woman without showing surprise.

The young butcher stopped sharpening his knife and took a long look at Melanie, who took a long look back. They were about the same age and the annoyance Michael felt surprised him. Was he being possessive?

The woman was now writing down an address and directions as to how to get to her mother-in-law. She lived on the family farm, some five kilometres from St. Aubin on the Sisteron-Manosque road. A track took you straight to the farm. You could see it from the road, a long low black barn, very old. The house was behind that.

Everyone thanked everybody else, they all shook hands and then left.

* * *

He followed the woman's directions and drove out of the village; second right after the crossroads, over the bridge along the road of poplars and sure enough there it was, a long low black barn with a sagging tiled roof at the end of a track.

He turned onto the track and bumped his way towards the farm. Orchards on either side, cows, the inevitable dog barking, the smell of pigs. A clever family, they obviously grew their own meat, slaughtered it and churned it out as salami.

He stopped the car behind a rusty tractor and both got out. Emma was sound asleep, not a murmur, not a movement. It almost worried him.

'Is she all right? She hasn't moved.'

Melanie leaned over her and put her

fingers close to the little nose and mouth.

'She's breathing.'

The farmhouse was a disappointment. It was modern. It was clearly a disappointment to Melanie, presumably because all things modern suggested that old things had been discarded. It annoyed him because the modern bungalow was totally unaesthetic and in France he expected things to be visually acceptable.

The bungalow had an ugly red roof on grey stone walls with aluminium framed windows, and inside, he sensed, it would have garish wallpaper and wrought iron spiders from a Costa Brava holiday. The television aerial on top of it all promised they would draw a total blank.

But he was wrong.

Madame Jules Lanotte was tall, with brassy blonde hair; she wore a white and blue polka dot dress and high-heeled white shoes. Sixty, sixty-five, she didn't belong to the farm, but she certainly belonged to the bungalow.

She greeted them both with a radiant smile of instant recognition, which was disconcerting. It was as though she had

107

known they were coming.

'Ma belle-fille m'a téléphoné,' she said, which explained everything. 'Vous faites des recherches historiques n'est-ce pas?'

They went in and were overcome by the smell of the lavender air spray she must have just used.

It was clear that as a widow she had inherited money and built herself this small bungalow where she lived out the life she had always wanted to live. It made no sense at all that this woman had a sense of history, but she showed them into a small study at the back where the walls were hung heavily with pictures of all the kings and queens of France.

Madame Lanotte chatted away about this and that, opened a desk drawer and brought out a cardboard box.

'Voici tous les documents de ma famille, qui retournent jusqu' au dix-huitième siècle.'

She handed it to Melanie who put it on the table and opened it.

Her eyes grew wider at the smell of the old pieces of paper. She went through various pictures and letters quickly and, as though she knew exactly what she was looking for, picked out a letter written in old script.

Madame Lanotte explained what the letter was and he translated for Melanie.

'It was apparently received by her great-great-aunt from a friend of a certain Jaume Lanotte, a corporal in Napoleon's army . . . ' He paused for a moment, realizing what he was saying. 'It was written from Tavira, Portugal, dated 1813.'

'Portugal? Can you read it for me, what does it say?'

She handed Michael the letter and he instantly realized he would not only have trouble in translating the old French, but have difficulty in reading the script.

'J'ai une copie,' said Madame Lanotte, 'tapée a la machine.'

She looked through the papers and found the typed transcript. It was much easier to read and the modern meanings of the old French words had been added in brackets.

Madame Lanotte asked them whether they would like a drink, a coffee, a liqueur, and Michael accepted a small cognac, Melanie a glass of mineral water.

He sat down and read the letter through, then translated it slowly.

My Dear Aunt,

Thanks be to God I am alive and well after three years of hardship and living with death for as long.

You will have heard by now that we suffered a defeat at the hands of the Spanish and English at Salamanca on the peninsula.

Things have been bad for us ever since.

With Jaume and Barrault I escaped capture and we fled south. Not till we reached the heat of Andalucia did we feel safe for there they did not know of the war. We were housed by a family of gypsies who were Christianly kind and believed in the Virgin Mary. But near Granada we were mercilessly attacked by local troops and Jaume, who lost his bad leg following our escape, was murdered.

I have a gold chain he wore round his

neck at the time of his death; it was given him by one of the gypsies. Please tell his sister it is for her and I am bringing it. He also had a cross which I buried with him. Barrault and I gave him a Christian burial in a small wood next to the cemetery of the village of Huejelar near Alhama, and marked his grave with a wooden cross.

I am awaiting a merchant ship bound for Marseilles and should be with you within three months.

I hope Barrault, from whom I parted company at Cadiz, will be home soon as well.

God be with you. Your loving nephew,

Pierrot.

Melanie listened intently and looked well pleased; when Michael had finished she opened her bag and to his surprise brought out a small black leather case from its depths. It was an expensive Japanese miniature camera with flashlight attachment. She placed the original letter and the typed copy side by side on the floor, stood above them, aimed and took several shots.

She was as fully equipped as an industrial spy.

The next hour or so was spent being polite to Madame Lanotte who asked Melanie many questions about her research work and how much it cost to trace ancestors, and it then occurred to Michael that somehow, along the complicated lines of family branches, he was related to this woman. He wasn't sure he liked the idea at all.

As they bid her goodbye on the threshold of the new bungalow, Melanie asked whether they could have a look around the farm as she was always interested in old buildings. The woman said she could do what she liked; the barn was even older than Pierrot's letter and no doubt the young man who had been murdered in Spain had worked in it. She apologized with a certain disdain for not accompanying them, saying that she never set foot within the farm, it was such a smelly, dirty place. Considering her wealth had come from the hams and offal of the pigs that had been reared in those confines, Michael thought it a little ungracious of her. The barn was really old and massive, the atmosphere as silent and peaceful as a cathedral. Sunlight filtered through holes in the roof and Melanie stood right in the middle of a ray, spotlighted like a golden-haired angel.

'There's something in here which matters,' she said, looking around.

'How do you mean?'

'There's something in here, something hidden away in here, which should mean something to you.'

'To *me*?'

'Yes. Whatever else, Michael, let your mind take you where it wants to go. The old saying, taking you where your steps lead you, is valid. You're being inhibited, you are being drawn to something but you're resisting.'

He looked at her and was surprised to see she had her eyes closed, her voice had changed a little to a more authoritative, deeper tone.

'Are you all right?' he asked.

'Just go, Michael. Just let yourself go.

Don't worry about me, it's too important.' She just stood there, rigid, her eyes still tightly shut as though she were trying to get into a trance.

'Go where you feel like going, Michael, don't hesitate, it may be that you want to get out of here, so just go . . . ' she said insistently.

He hesitated, thinking of leaving by the way they had come in, but instead actually did as she had suggested and headed for the small doorway at the end which intrigued him.

Away from her he suddenly felt freer, and then an urgent need overtook him to get out of the barn through that far doorway, so that he quickened his steps. It was the light and the promise of the blue sky and fresh air. He was feeling enclosed, claustrophobic, though it hardly made sense in such a large space.

He reached the doorway and found it didn't lead anywhere at all, not out into the open anyway. It just led to an old pig sty, open to the sky, which accounted for the light, but it was an addition to the barn, stacked full of old firewood and the throw-aways of years of farm implements; old spades, scythes, a plough, cart wheels. Some of the shapes were intriguing, the workmanship of one particular piece of carved wood, probably the front of a door panel, was quite beautiful, and as he reached out to touch it he had the quite exceptional sensation that he had to push the panel, push it gently so he did and it gave way, slipped down, revealing behind it what looked like a straight stick, the handle of a rake perhaps, only thicker.

'That's it!' Melanie shouted from behind him, 'That's it!'

He turned round to look at her. She was quite pale, and her eyes were staring at the rake handle.

'What's *it*?'

'Bring it out.'

'What, this?' He reached for the rake handle, pulled it and realized it wasn't a rake at all; it had a small cross bar joining two handles of wood, well worn, smooth, as though held for years. It was a crutch.

As he grabbed hold of it to pull it out, his heart sank, the full meaning of what he had found dawned on him. Jaume

Lanotte's crutch? Impossible.

'It's his, isn't it?' Melanie said, 'Just hold it and close your eyes and tell me what you feel, what you see, what you sense.'

He glanced around to make sure no one else was around and closed his eyes. Then he let out a gasp as an agonising pain cut right through the top of his right leg above the knee. He opened his eyes expecting to see a manic Melanie swinging a knife or a scythe at him, but she was standing some distance away and his leg was untouched.

'Jesus!' he said, dropping the crutch.

'What? What happened?'

'I just had this terrible pain in my leg.'

'You're so psychic, Michael, you could probably predict earthquakes. Pick it up again.'

'Not if it's going to give me pains like that, thank you.'

'Go on, just pick it up, it could lead us to . . . ' She stopped.

'Lead us to what?'

'Lead us to him.'

'To him? He's in Spain, buried in some

116

remote Andalusian village!'

'Exactly. Pick it up, hold my hand. I'll take the pain.'

'What do you mean?'

'Please, Michael, just do it!'

He stooped down to pick it up, at the same time taking her hand. Her grip was incredibly strong. It wasn't a small girl's grip at all, it was vice-like and to his astonishment the crutch started moving in his hand; it started shaking and she started shaking and he was caught between the two. He looked at her, her eyes were closed, she was gritting her teeth and the crutch was shaking. It was like being caught between two electrodes, and he dropped it.

She let out a long sigh, opened her eyes, mopped her brow and smiled at him.

'My God, we've got so much power between us, we could conquer the world! Do you realize what power we've got?'

'No, I don't,' he answered.

'Oh, Michael, you're so innocent about our human capabilities. You have no idea what we can do. Don't you realize that psychic functioning is normal, it's just that it's been so long repressed that we don't believe in it. Our minds, for generations, have been programmed to think it can't happen. But it can.'

'What can?'

'See into the future, see into the past. Our powers of clairvoyance, of remote viewing, of receiving clear images of future events, precognition, of extra-sensory perception are infinite. What do you think you're doing right now?'

He shrugged his shoulders.

'You have powers in you which probably no other human being has, you can see as far back into the past along your generation line as you wish, and you can probably see the same distance into the future. You also have incredible powers of ESP, just look what happened with that crutch. You can't go on living the way you do, you owe it to humanity to develop yourself.'

She was so intense, this little girl, standing in front of him in the middle of the barn lecturing him, reading him the riot act.

He led her out, holding her hand and the crutch, not feeling anything, and went into the farmyard.

Passing the bungalow Melanie knocked on the door to ask Madame Lanotte if they could keep the crutch. She said 'Of course' in a way which told them she clearly thought them mad and was disappointed that such knowledgeable people should take an interest in such a disgusting piece of wood which probably had the disease of whatever cripple it had belonged to.

They got into the car.

'Where to?' Michael asked.

'Home,' Melanie said.

He started the engine and felt relief at hearing the sound of something he could control. 'We can conquer' had been out of character with the soft, sweet, gentle girl he had got to know. If she was right and he had to open himself up to his own awareness, then his intuition about her was not so much to be aware but to be wary.

6

When they got home Michael was so tired that he took the elevator to the first floor. It was admitting defeat, admitting that he was not as young and sprightly as he used to be, which he didn't like, but as he hardly ever had any exercise he could hardly expect to be always in trim. Going up and down the stairs helped, but tonight he really felt weak at the knees and was pleased that he had kept up this expensive folly for taking invalids up and down.

He showered and put on his bathrobe and joined Melanie in the kitchen for a snack she was preparing after feeding Emma and putting her to bed.

'Shall we take it all upstairs and relax a bit with some music?' he suggested.

Melanie put everything on two trays and they carried one each to the elevator. He put his down on the floor to close the gates.

After they had watched the news on television and he was deciding what to listen to, Melanie cautiously asked whether she could play him one of Sarah's tapes. Michael felt he could not refuse.

Happy, she went down to her room and came back with the cassette recorder and switched it on.

Sarah's voice, with a hard metallic tone to it, came through.

'I am in the open, in a vineyard, it is very hot, the sky is pale blue and I am not alone. There are old women in the distance whom I do not like . . . but I am comforted by their presence, for I feel I am in some kind of danger. The danger is threatened by three men, soldiers, French soldiers, one of whom is crippled. They have been staying just outside the village with the gitanes. The cripple wants something from me and eyes the gold cross around my neck and the gold chain. They are poor, these soldiers, they are renegades, and as they come towards me I hold onto my gold cross, I want it to bring me luck, or bring them ill-luck, for in their eyes I see that they are not kind, that the cripple is evil ... and I know that something awful is going to happen ... something ... awful is going to hap ... '

The voice stopped. The tape was silent. Melanie switched it off.

'Is that all?'

'Yes. I have fourteen recordings of that same memory and that is the longest. She could never remember more.'

She looked at him questioningly. 'You haven't had a similar dream?'

'No.'

He could hardly keep his eyes open, he wanted to sleep, he was desperately tired.

'I'm sorry,' he said at last, 'but I'm exhausted, I must go to bed.'

Quite unthinkingly he got up and bent down to give her a brief goodnight kiss. It took them both by surprise, but he was too tired to react, too tired to care what it meant.

He'd sort everything out in the morning.

★ ★ ★

Melanie brought him breakfast at eleven and sat on the end of the bed looking at him, waiting for him to awaken fully

He sat up, pyjama-less as always, not caring this time what effect it had on her. She was no longer timid, the relationship was getting more domestic.

'I would like to go to Spain as soon as possible,' she said. 'We have enough material now to find Jaume Lanotte's body.'

He looked at her in disbelief.

'Jaume Lanotte was buried with the girl's cross,' she started to explain. 'If we can find that cross, we can find out who she was, and maybe link her with Immaculada Almargo who married William Fainhope. There must be a connection.'

'What are you going to do? Disinter him?'

'It may not be necessary. It depends on how powerful your sensory perceptions are.'

'What do we do with Emma this time? We can't take her to Spain with us.'

'I thought I could take her to England

to Sarah's parents-in-law; they'd love to have her, and she's no trouble now she doesn't need her early morning feed.'

'When would you go?'

'Whenever it suits you, suits them.'

Spain. He'd always wanted to go to Spain. A real holiday with a purpose. It would be easier to go now before he'd started setting up in business again.

'I'll ring them up and see what they think of the idea,' he said, reaching for the telephone.

David's mother answered and was delighted to hear from him and all about Emma, and even more delighted when he asked her if she could take care of her for a month.

'It gives me a reason for living,' she said, and suggested that Melanie should fly in at the end of the week; they would meet her at Heathrow.

Michael booked the air tickets for Melanie and Emma and on the day drove them to the airport. He sat on the restaurant balcony sipping a beer, he watched the 'plane take off over the sea and get smaller in the sky, and tried to

124

sort out his feelings.

He felt some regret at their departure, a vacuum.

When he got back to the empty house he realized he had got used to Melanie. He liked her, he wanted her help, wanted to believe all she believed, wanted to understand her more.

He went up to her room. He lay down on her bed and turned to look at his own reflection in the mirror.

Disquieting.

Why did she have the mirror there? Was it just to look at herself? He suspected it might be for something more diabolical. But what? And he still didn't know her well enough simply to ask her. Their domestic intimacy had not developed that much.

Could he perhaps find out with his supposed powers? Could he close his eyes and travel into some land of great revelation? What if he went into a dream, a memory? Was he frightened, then? Was he afraid of being psychic?

He got up and opened her cupboard. The crutch was hanging there on a hook and he had a terrible urge to touch it, but remembered the pain.

How could he dismiss that pain?

What if he touched other objects then? His grandmother's jewellery box? Why had an image of that just flashed through his mind? It was downstairs on his desk, a black metal and ormolu casket lined with red silk in which he kept a gold magnifying glass but nothing else.

He went downstairs.

Six o'clock in the evening. The depressing time of day, the high temperature time in hospitals, dusk, sunset, the hour he disliked most.

He opened the jewellery box, took out the magnifying glass, then sat well back in the swivel chair holding the box on his knees, his eyes closed.

He let his thumb feel the surface of the casket, the embossed centaur and nymphs. It was quite a new casket, not an antique, sold in hundreds in the States around 1915. His grandmother had kept her jewellery in it. She had bought it in a gift shop on Long Island; she was wearing a blue dress. She was buying it to cheer herself up. She felt guilty holding it, paying for it with a brand-new dollar bill from a string purse. Henry would be angry.

Who was Henry?

He opened his eyes and realized he was coming back into the room from very far away. It was that totally unexpected feeling, the coming back, the awakening from a deep but short sleep, yet not.

Henry? Who was Henry? Where did that name come from?

His grandmother Louise, his grandfather Michael, Aunt Lizzy, Uncle Harry . . .

Uncle Harry! Uncle Henry! His grandmother's brother. Why should she be afraid of him?

Because Henry had given her the money to buy something else, something for him because he was unable to go out. He was ill in bed with typhoid. He died from it. Hence the guilt. And he knew all this. He *knew* it. It wasn't day-dreaming, it wasn't fantasy. He knew it. Somewhere in his head there were all these memories. Other people's memories, inherited memories.

How did he bring it on? And how could he project himself, forward, see into the future? Would it work by holding something else, something new, something that had no history?

He went into the drawing room to look for something suitable, took a small Raulk off the wall, a pen-and-ink sketch, placed the frame on his knees and put both palms flat down on the glass, then closed his eyes.

'Vibrate then, dammit!' he said to himself, and sat like that for quite some time feeling nothing at all but a tickling sensation in his spine and in his left leg where cramp and pins-and-needles were beginning to set in.

Then he got a quite ridiculous image of Raulk, painting an electric storm up in the mountains. He was standing back from the canvas on an easel and hurling paint at it as lightning streaked across the sky. It was so ludicrous that he smiled to himself, opened his eyes and stood up. Obviously his logical subconscious was sending him a message — waste your time imagining that you're psychic and you'll dream up anything.

As he hung the sketch back up on the wall, the telephone rang.

It was Melanie, from Suffolk, with David's parents and Emma, telling him that all was well and she would be returning on Monday.

To please her he mentioned his experiment that he'd been trying to see into the future but did not know how to go about it.

'Predictions come to you. Holding a modern sketch won't help at all unless Raulk was going through a state of anxiety when he was doing it.'

And he didn't realize what she had said until he'd put the phone down.

He hadn't mentioned the nature of his experiment. How could she possibly have known what he had been doing?

★   ★   ★

When he went to meet Melanie at the airport, he waited as usual at the customs barrier. He was happy to be there, going through the qualms of expectancy, would she be there, was it the right flight, could she have missed it?

The London passengers started filtering through and among them he suddenly saw, quite clearly, a girl who looked just like Sarah. Younger, dressed in a peach-coloured gown with long skirt, quite out of keeping with all the other passengers, as though she were a bridesmaid at a wedding. He lost sight of her as Melanie appeared, waving at him, pointing luggage already coming through on the moving belt. They greeted each other with a hug and kisses on both cheeks.

'I've brought lots of things with me this time, all Sarah's recording equipment, which was at the farm.'

A porter helped him put the two speakers, recording unit and amplifier in the boot.

'I've also brought you something special,' she said, obviously very excited by a present she had found for him.

Back at the house, in her room again, she unzipped a hold-all and handed him a flat book-like package neatly wrapped in gift paper.

'It's not my birthday or anything,' he said.

'It doesn't have to be.'

Inside the wrapping was something in tissue paper, it felt like a small frame, an antique frame perhaps to put Emma's photograph in?

It was in fact a woodcut, the portrait of an old man with a beard, bulging eyes, wearing a skull cap.

'Michel de Nostredamme, your ancestor,' she explained.

'It's very beautiful, where did you get it?'

'In Paris, two years ago. I was going to give it to Sarah when I had come up with the proof that they were related. I thought I'd give it to you, now.'

'Without the proof?'

'Oh, no. With the proof. At least nearly. I have another present for you.'

She brought out another gift-wrapped package, another picture it seemed, larger, and handed it to him.

'You're spoiling me,' he said.

'You can cope.'

He had difficulty in opening it, so she

found some scissors and cut the paper ribbon. Inside was more tissue paper, another frame. It was a poem written in spidery shaky handwriting on very thin, very old parchment.

> *Auprès d'oliviers et nudité étoile*
> *Parent du vingt et unième, unique au monde.*
> *Divine, sa mère bientôt sous voile.*
> *Père mort d'une chute étroite et profonde.*

He'd seen it in her bedside book, but said nothing. Could this be the original?

'What does it mean?' he asked.

'It's a Nostradamus quatrain which I found in your grandfather's diary. Sarah had it.'

He remembered now. Shortly before she had left for England to get married he had given Sarah a box of old family documents he had never valued.

'Your grandfather, Michael D'Artson, must have been aware of the connection. It was he who changed his name by deed poll to D'Artson, to read Nostra D backwards. This quatrain must have come into his possession.'

'But what does it mean?'

'It's a prediction,' she said, 'about Emma. The first line *Near olive trees and nudity by starlight* is at first baffling, but if *étoile* is separated to read *et toile*, and 'toile' being the French for canvas is taken to mean a painting, we get — *Near olive trees and nudity by painting*, which must refer to this house near Renoir's studio where he painted nudes among the olive trees. *Parent of the twenty first, unique on earth* refers to Sarah, parent of Emma who, according to calculations could be the twenty-first in line from Nostradamus and therefore probably superclairvoyant, thus unique. *Divine, her mother soon seen under veil:* Sarah again, prophecy of her death soon after Emma's birth. *Father dead of narrow and deep fall:* clearly David, Emma's father, killed in the 'plane crash.'

'So according to this Emma is unique and super-clairvoyant,' he said.

'Maybe. But until the chart is completed we can't be certain she's the twenty-first.'

* * *

They set off for Spain the next day as though for a touring holiday, but the boot of the car was loaded with recording equipment and the place of honour on the back seat was reserved for the crutch, now wrapped in a plastic sheet.

Cannes, St Raphael, St Maxim, St Tropez; they went out of their way in Toulon searching for the postcard hospital but learned it had been pulled down. They drove through Montpellier where Nostradamus had studied medicine when he was nineteen and where according to Melanie's chart, his illegitimate daughter, Reyniere, had been born.

They bypassed Perpignan, then they went across the border into Spain down to Figueras where, after, a day's drive, they stayed the night.

The following day they took the motorway straight down to Valencia, but bored with the monotony of the straight road decided to cut across country to Granada via Albacota and Jaen. After two hours of seemingly endless driving on a road which hadn't been repaired for over ten years, dodging potholes, keeping to the middle where it was less bumpy, aware that the petrol gauge was low and that they might not reach another petrol station before they ran out, they were greeted, five kilometres or so outside Albacota, by a huge billboard proclaiming the civilized wonders of the brand new Hotel Claveles.

The advertisements became more numerous as they got nearer the town and they were delighted at the thought of stopping in a place of super luxury with the promise of a swimming pool, air conditioning and everything else that two weary travellers needed.

The Hotel Claveles, however, was not to be opened to the public for another week. The other two respectable places were full and, in desperation, they finally found two small rooms in a pension which hinted at cockroaches and mosquitoes, but which was by then welcome, the mind not caring as long as the body could be rested.

After a rest in the comparative coolness

of his back room, a trickle of water from the metal rose that called itself a shower and a generous rubbing with eau de Cologne, Michael felt better, even hungry.

With Melanie, he was happy to wander the streets of this strange unfinished town till they eventually found a bar where they offered tapas of smoked ham, pickled anchovies, tortilla and other snacks, a decanter of red wine per person and a great deal of shouting. He would have preferred to sit down at a linen-covered table and be waited on, but after the first few mouthfuls of calamares and garban-zos, he was pleased that Melanie, determined to savour the non-touristic side of the country, had forced him to be more adventurous.

After a black coffee that promised to keep him awake all night, they walked a little bit more.

As they turned a corner they found themselves in front of the new Hotel Claveles, with its eight storeys of polished marble balconies and as yet unfinished drive-in road, flanked by newly planted palm trees which were understandably the pride of the town.

Tiredness from the day's travel then overcame them and they mutually decided to go to bed. Back at the pension they went to their separate rooms as they had in the Figueras hotel after bidding each other a polite goodnight.

Michael undressed completely, got in between the coarse white sheets, and allowed himself to consider the idea of conquering Melanie and slipping between her freckled thighs. Since appearing in the nude in the Renoir garden she had behaved in an exemplary way, and certainly he had never had a hint of her having a boy friend.

Despite the coffee his eyes felt heavy with sleep and when he closed them he promptly fell asleep. He was, however, awakened in the dead of night by the unexpected sound of a pneumatic drill. It was incredibly loud, then not just one but several drills shattered the peace.

He could not believe it.

He switched on the light, looked at his watch, it was four in the morning. He went to the window. The pneumatic drills were incessant and the noise was coming from the direction of the new hotel. In the street below people were running seemingly silently towards the disturbance, the drills drowning all other sounds. A long black car, an ambulance, a lorry sped past. The jack-hammers went on.

He was wide awake, really wide awake and curious. He slipped on his shirt, his trousers, his canvas shoes and took the stairs down in the darkness of the hotel.

There were no noises in the building, nothing, no one else had been awakened.

Michael went out into the street which was now deserted and silent. He went towards the new hotel; no drills could be heard, not a car, not a person.

He turned the corner and gasped at the horrific sight. The Hotel Claveles was a heap of rubble, a grey mass of twisted metal and stone, a balcony hung from a thread of a girder and people were frantically digging with their hands. As he stood there, rooted to the spot, he watched as two men strained to shift a massive cement block under which was the crushed and bloody body of a man in pyjamas. Michael stared at the man's expression of hideous accusation; it seemed to be saying, 'Why didn't you tell me this would happen?'

Michael turned away, wanting to help but not sure what to do. He glanced up at the overhanging third floor, saw it shudder and looked at the people working below. He cried out, shouted, but his voice, as though in a fearful dream, made no noise at all.

Then the storey collapsed, fell as one block sending a cloud of thick dust over everything. The jack-hammers that had started again were suddenly silenced. He looked around, heard his own voice wailing, realized that he was quite alone in the middle of the street in front of the Hotel Claveles, untouched, unmarred, glorious with its name on a brand-new flag fluttering in the breeze from a golden pole on the roof.

He saw that he was dressed, thank God, in his shirt, his trousers, his canvas shoes. He had sleepwalked obviously, and dreamed it all. Smiling apologetically to no one, he walked back to the pension. The front door was ajar, he found the light switch in the darkness and climbed the five floors not wanting to disturb anyone by using the elevator; he reached his room and got onto the bed. He had slept-walked for the first time in his life. He had dreamed and walked in his sleep. He lay down, eased off his shoes and closed his eyes. That man, that half body, the crushed chest, the blood, the sound of drills had all been so real. He had experienced it fully, even the smells, the dust, the heat. For a moment he thought of waking Melanie up to tell her, but what for? He had had a bad dream, it could not have been a memory.

He next awoke to find Melanie shaking him, quite hard, her anxious young face looking down at him, her long red hair brushing his face.

'Are you all right?'

'Yes, of course. What time is it?'

'Half past nine. Didn't you undress?'

'Yes . . . that is . . . no.' He wasn't going to tell her. He didn't want to go into any explanations right now, didn't want an analysis. 'I guess I just went straight to sleep. We'd better get on, hadn't we?'

The memory of the dream faded as they drove to Jaen. It came back whenever they crossed a town and the dusty roads and unfinished buildings came into sight. They had lunch at a supposedly expensive restaurant, a cellar decorated with hunting trophies, stuffed deers' heads, shotguns and hunting pouches. The food was good and unaccountably cheap. It made him feel better. Filling the car up with petrol and checking the oil and the battery had helped him recover a sense of normality. The day-to-day routine of modern living had its good points. He needed reassurance.

* * *

By the time they got to Granada, Melanie was suffering from the heat and for the first time ever he wished the car had an air conditioning system. With all the windows open and driving at a steady eighty it was still hot.

The main road out of Granada to Malaga was straight and smooth and a delight compared to the rough going from Jaen, but the turning to Alhama de Granada took them onto an uncertain surface again.

The village of Huejelar, their destination, was not on any modern maps. Melanie, however, had found an old one where it was marked, six kilometres due west of Alhama.

She had it all worked out. They would go to the area and camp there and walk around till Michael got a reaction with the crutch. She felt absolutely certain he would.

He had never been a great camper, had never in fact camped in his life, and did not in the least relish the idea of spending a night out in the open. He drove through the seemingly deserted village of Huejelar and parked in what might once have been a main square in front of a chapel. A door was open in one of the low whitewashed cortijos and he suspected that it might be the main village shop.

Melanie got out of the car and walked straight in, he followed after stretching his legs a little.

Behind the bar there was a woman who eyed them both with great suspicion. The place was virtually empty. There were two folding chairs, a bottle on the only shelf, a plastic beer crate behind the bar, another chair, a doorway leading to a room beyond and a Fanta advertisement on the wall next to a faded '103' Cognac calendar.

'Un vino blanco,' he heard Melanie ask.

Strange young lady. Shy on most occasions, but when the atmosphere was positively oppressive, she was cool and calm and in command.

'What do you want, Michael?'

'I'll have the same. Any ice?'

'You're joking.'

The woman brought out two tiny but very clean glasses which she wiped again with the inside of her thumb; she found a bottle of white wine under the counter and poured out two tots.

They both drank them down too quickly and had to ask for more.

The wine was a trifle acid, but Michael needed it. What he really wanted was a long Scotch and soda with ice.

Melanie took from her bag a piece of paper on which were written the various directions mentioned in the Pierrot letter, and checked a word in the dictionary she carried.

'El cemeterio?' Melanie asked the woman, but got no answer. So far not a word had come from her mouth. Strangers were clearly unwanted.

From outside came the sound of hooves slowly clip-clopping and Michael glanced out of the doorway to see a muleteer leading a weary animal which looked like Don Quixote's Rosinante. The man made a noise and the mule came to a dead stop. He tied its halter to a ring in the wall. They could have been in a Western.

The man took his time coming in, staring at the car as though it had no right to be there.

'Buena . . . ' he said to no one in particular.

The woman behind the bar brought

out a tall glass and from under the counter a dewy bottle of cold beer. She had an ice box there.

The man gulped down the cold beer and Michael wondered whether he should have one. Cold beer on that wine? It was what he wanted.

'Una cervesa,' he said. 'Would you like one?'

Melanie nodded.

'Dos.'

More clip-clopping, more hooves, and outside two other muleteers, covered with dust, paused to look at the car. Younger men, studying the machine with a twinge of envy perhaps or just curious at this hint of the space age.

They came in. 'Buena . . . ' they said, and slapped the older man affectionately on the back.

The woman poured one of them a beer, the other an anisseco. They started talking amongst themselves in a language which was incomprehensible, Andalusian no doubt.

The older man sat down on a chair and rolled himself a cigarette with tobacco from a tin, his gnarled fingers expertly twisting the paper. The two younger men looked at Melanie when they could, their eyes making it clear that they thought she might be better if she had a little more meat on her, but it was nice all the same to have a female in their midst. One of them made a remark about her and the woman behind the bar chortled rudely.

Using her femininity to full advantage, Melanie asked the men where the cemetery was. One of them moved closer and looked at her, his nostrils flaring on smelling her scent. It unsettled him.

'El cemeterio? Por que?' He heaved his shoulders up questioningly. Why would anyone want to go there?

'Conosco . . . ?' she asked.

'Claro. Ahi . . . ' he said, pointing out of the door.

Taking the opportunity the man grabbed her elbow and led her out of the door. Michael followed. They went out past the car parked in the middle of the dusty square and the man pointed due north at a line of cypress trees. Melanie nodded and thanked him.

'It's over there, about half a mile,' she said confidently. She then took out the old map she had, studied the landscape and said, 'Yes, those cypresses there, are these here, the chapel behind us is here on the map, and that dip must have been where there was a river.'

They all went back into the bar and Michael offered the men a drink, they all had another beer but when he came to pay the woman made it clear it had been taken care of.

'He's paid, we're his guests,' Melanie explained. 'Don't insist or he'll be insulted.'

They shook hands all round and strolled back to the car.

The track down was not good. Michael drove in first gear along the ridges on either side of a deep gulley dug by the winter rain. It was mule country. What was he doing there with a car, and how the hell was he going to get back? There was no way he was going to be able to reverse.

At last they came to a clearing, a field, and he drove onto the flat rocky earth. It was the end of the road, from now on they would have to walk.

They both got out and looked around. They were surrounded by vines, stunted and gnarled but miraculous considering the barrenness of the ground.

He looked back at Huejelar and was struck by the shape of the buildings and the little bell tower on the chapel. It was so familiar that it made all the anxieties of being a stranger in a foreign land disappear. He suddenly felt at home and wanted to walk back to the village, but not along the track he had just taken. There was another, farther to the left down in the valley.

Curious to know why he felt there was a track there, he left Melanie and walked through the vineyard and down the slope. There, sure enough, was the track with the little white stone sanctuary which marked the entrance to the old cemetery. Why did he know this?

Melanie came up behind him.

'You've been here before, haven't you?'

'Yes,' he admitted.

'For God's sake don't hold yourself

back. Walk, go where you feel comfortable.'

He stood there for a moment longer then, intrigued, walked on down the slope and stopped on the track itself. To the right, towards the village, was safety. To the left definite anxiety, even fear.

'I feel something very strong from the left. Something unpleasant must have happened.'

'Let's go. Let's go back along the track.'

Michael was reluctant to do so. He had no idea what he feared, but it was there, a very strong feeling of unpleasantness.

'You're entering anxiety traces,' Melanie said.

Instinctively he looked up the hill.

'They were up there.'

'Who were up there?' Melanie asked gently.

'The men who were protecting us.' What was he talking about?

'Who were 'us'?'

'My aunt,' he said. 'Concepcion, Esperanza and Rosario were there too.'

'Stay right there, please, Michael, I'm going back to the car to get the crutch.'

149

He sat down on the hard earth and looked at the furrows between the grape vines. They were so familiar. He reached out and instinctively started picking the hard, green, unripened grapes. This is what he had been doing here in this field God knew how many years ago.

He got up and walked along one line of vines, then crossed over to another and caught his breath. The three men had been right there in front of him and his aunt and cousins were to the left, staring.

Melanie came back, and stood next to him. He was pleased.

'I was a young girl here, my name was Maria Dolores,' he said. 'I was raped by a cripple, who stole my little gold cross.'

Melanie handed him the crutch.

He was so tired suddenly that he didn't flinch at the thought of the pain it might give him, and to his surprise nothing happened.

But it started shaking. It seemed to have a life of its own. He closed his eyes again and felt the crutch pulling him away from where he was.

'Is it pulling you in any direction?' he

heard Melanie ask in the far distance.

'Yes.'

'Towards those trees? Hold it with both hands, use it like a water diviner.'

'What will happen?' he asked.

'If Jaume Lanotte is buried around here, that's where it will take you. You're getting vibrations from two people who were united somewhere here and who both experienced something horrible. We must find out what, and where.'

7

They were walking, with some difficulty, along the shallow furrows of the vineyard, holding the crutch in front of them as though it were a plough.

He wondered whether he and Melanie could be seen from Huejelar, whether the muleteers and the woman were watching them.

Then he stopped.

'What's happening?' Melanie asked, thinking Michael had sensed something.

'How did you get into the car for the crutch? I locked all the doors and the key's in my pocket.'

'You didn't lock all the doors, the back one my side was open.'

He was sure it wasn't, but went on walking.

Then he stopped again.

'Why would a one-legged French soldier be engaged to fight in Napoleon's army in Spain?'

'He hadn't lost his leg when he came to fight in Spain.'

'What's this crutch then?'

'This crutch was used at home by Jaume Lanotte to recover from the wound he suffered when a cannon fell on him during the battle of Wagram. For a long time this crutch was Jaume's closest friend. That's why you're getting such good vibrations from it.'

'Why would it have vibrations down here in Spain?'

'It's like a homing device, Michael,' she explained patiently. 'Possessions become part of the person to whom they belong. That's why I want to find that cross. The object doesn't always have to have lived *through* experiences with people, it has to have been prized by that person. If I wanted to be led to you I would hold your signet ring.'

He glanced at his signet ring. He never took it off except to wash his hands.

'Didn't that letter say something about him losing his leg though?'

'Yes. But after Salamanca. Why are you so worried about his leg?'

'Because I don't feel I have a right one at all, it's completely numb.'

The crutch now started vibrating in his hands like the steering wheel of an unbalanced vehicle. If he moved it away from its present point of direction it would stop, and Melanie would move it back on.

'I'm only testing it,' he said.

'It's like a dog, it can lose the scent.'

'How do you know about these things?'

'Don't talk now, just follow the direction of the vibrations.'

They were in the shadow of the hill now, down in the dip heading for a grove of eucalyptus trees. Melanie held his wrist tightly. He wasn't sure whether she was taking his pulse as well as getting a reaction. Whatever she was doing it was strange indeed, and then the pain in his right leg began to make itself felt, not like the previous one, just at the top, ten or so inches above the knee.

'Up the hill, straight up,' Melanie said, urging him on when he hesitated. It hurt so much now that he was limping.

They got to the top of the hill. A

well-worn path led straight down to a dried-up stream which disappeared into the grove of eucalyptus trees.

Quite suddenly the crutch was jerked up so forcefully that it swung him round as though someone had got hold of it and wanted to wrench it out of his hands. At the same time he felt the excruciating pain in his leg and to his astonishment collapsed in a heap as the crutch was hurled some twenty feet down the path towards the eucalyptus grove.

The pain went and he turned round to see Melanie standing stock still with her eyes wide open, breathing heavily through clenched teeth. She had gone white, and was perspiring and shaking uncontrollably.

He got to his feet to help her but the moment he came between her and the crutch it was like stepping across an electric field, and he had to go back.

He went round her and as he got closer to her again she turned and opened her mouth.

'Putain de béquille!' she said in a deep rasping voice, her eyes now tightly closed.

Frightened, Michael slapped her hard across the face. She opened her eyes immediately, shook her head and took a very deep breath, her lips trembling.

'You must never do that. Never. It can kill me,' and, as though winded, she took more deep breaths.

'I'm sorry,' he said, 'I just don't know how to handle these situations. I don't know what's happening, what you're doing.'

'I'm a go-between, just accept it. Everything is working through me. He's buried in there among the trees.'

Michael looked at the trees. They were swaying in the soft breeze, reddish bronze in the evening sun. Nothing could have looked more peaceful or enchantingly cool.

'We'll picnic here,' Melanie said. 'We can't do anything till nightfall anyway.'

'What do you intend to do?'

'Dig him up. He's buried with the cross.'

'How can we dig up a body? We haven't even got a spade.'

'Yes we have. I put one in the plastic

156

sheet with the crutch.' She was a professional ghost hunter.

'What if we're seen?'

'We won't be.'

'I suppose you've got extra-sensory perception or some built-in radar system to ward off the curious?'

'Something like that,' she said, smiling sweetly. 'We'll leave the crutch where it is, go back to the car, get the picnic things and the spade and have a well-earned rest 'till nightfall.'

'What if someone sees the car? The village people know we're down here, won't they wonder what we're up to?'

'They won't be in the least bit interested.'

Leading the way back from the car with the picnic basket, the spade and her cassette recorder, anxious now to get into the shade and out of the burning sun, Michael looked out for the crutch but couldn't see it.

'The crutch has gone.'

Melanie was surprised.

She tried not to show it, but she was surprised.

'It must be in the trees.'

'How can it be? Nobody's been down here.'

'Things have a life of their own sometimes, you know.'

He didn't want to believe it.

He let her lead the way now, and as they reached the eucalyptus grove and stepped into the coolness of the shade, it was like entering a sacred place, silent as the grave, the rarefied atmosphere of a haunted area.

'It's here,' Melanie said, finding the crutch.

'He's under there, I expect,' she added.

'Why don't we start digging?' He asked it lightly, but couldn't see himself actually doing so.

'Because it's very hot and I'm hungry and thirsty.'

All he wanted to do was get on with whatever she wanted to do and get the hell out of it. He wasn't a bit hungry.

Melanie, cool and unperturbed, spread out the car rug and laid out all the food and drink for the picnic.

Michael sat down.

A few feet away, if he believed her, there was a body some few feet underground.

'I'm not entirely happy about this, you know,' he said.

'I know. But you will be. If you help me and we find the cross, you can sleep with me.'

It came out just like that. We'll do you a swap. Dig up the remains of a body and you can have mine.

He couldn't believe it.

'What did you say?' he asked.

'You heard. Ham, chicken with mayonnaise?' she offered, holding out a sandwich.

'I'm not hungry,' he said. 'Is there anything to drink?' He needed a drink.

'Iced tea. I don't think you should have any wine.'

'Don't you now?'

There was a limit to what he would take, and if he was going to spend the night digging, he was going to drink while doing so.

Melanie didn't try to stop him, but watched as Michael found the bottle of red wine in another bag and opened it. He poured himself out a good measure in a goblet, then took a chicken leg from a plastic box and dug his teeth into it. She had purchased all the food from a supermercado in Granada without his help. As far as catering went she was a genius.

'Earlier on you said you were a go-between.' said. 'What did you mean?'

'I'm a sort of transmitter.'

'Between the living and the dead?'

'There's no communication with the dead, as far as I know. All I do is create a field of energy in which people like you, who are psychic, can see traces of what has been. I am a force, a current if you like. You are a television receiver, the anxiety traces are the programme. I am the camera and transmitter.'

'Are there any happy traces?'

'Yes. You saw one yourself.'

'When?'

'At the airport when you met me last Sunday. Sarah. You saw Sarah as large as life coming through customs with me.'

'That was someone who looked like her.'

'No. It was her.'

'How do you know?'

'Because each time it happens I'm drained of energy.'

'It was Sarah's ghost then?'

'No. It was a trace. She was so pleased to see you last time she was there that she left a trace behind. When both of us happened to be there at the same time, the trace took shape, but only for you and me. Did you see what she was wearing?'

'Yes. A peach-coloured dress.'

'I saw her in a blue outfit, you see. Strange, isn't it? The peach dress was probably significant for you.'

'It was a bridesmaid's dress,' he said.

He couldn't remember at whose wedding she'd worn it but remembered that it was the first time he'd seen her looking so pretty and realized she was no longer a little girl.

'If we went back to the airport, could we recreate Sarah again and again?'

'No. The trace fades. It gets used up. Which is why ghosts, as they are called, are very seldom seen by more than one or two people. The trace is sapped. It's like a smell . . . open the window and it will disappear. Anxiety traces seem to be more potent and stay longer mainly because people block them off as soon as they feel them.'

He reached for the wine bottle and helped himself to another full goblet.

'So what happened along that path earlier on when your voice changed and you spoke French?'

'Did I?'

'You don't remember?'

'No. I'm not in control. I can only be used.'

'Who decides when to use you?'

'Nobody. It's like an electric storm. The two charged clouds are drawn together and the current passes from one to the other and there is an explosion.'

He looked at her for a long time. It was just possible that she was having him on, that the whole thing was some great inexplicable trick. Why she should want to do it he didn't know, but that she might be able to do it was probable. She might have thrown the crutch into the grove when he wasn't looking. She might certainly have imitated the deep French voice. What she could not have done, however, was cause him that pain in the right leg.

'I could well do with a cigar,' he said, hoping she would go and get him his cigar case which was in the car.

'Why don't you have one then?'

'They're in the car.'

'I'll get them.'

'No, don't bother,' he protested, mildly.

'I don't mind.'

He watched her as she got up and ambled off. She moved pleasingly.

He sipped his wine slowly and waited till she was at the top of the ridge, out of sight, then he got up, went over to the crutch lying in the grass and picked it up.

Absolutely nothing happened.

He had to have her as a catalyst then? Or was it all imagination? Was he going a little bit mad? Was it hypnosis of some kind?

He stuck the crutch under his arm and lifted his right leg, putting all his weight on the wood, took several steps, realizing how hard it was. He was about to make

163

sounds resembling Long John Silver, amused by what he was doing, when he sensed someone behind him.

He turned and gasped.

For a very brief moment he saw standing behind him the faint outline of a figure, bearded, but otherwise faceless, nodding approval, as though saying 'That's the way to do it, you've got it right first time.' It was all there in an expressionless face, then the pain came back like a stab, he dropped the crutch, lost his balance and stupidly fell to the ground.

The apparition had gone, he was completely alone. He looked towards the car but could not see Melanie.

He wanted her, he suddenly feared that she would never come back, then she appeared bobbing up and down over the brow of the hill, and he watched her coming, picking her way slowly along the vineyard furrows, holding the cigar box.

He would not tell her what had happened.

He tried to settle down, look relaxed, helped himself to more wine and toyed with a tomato while Melanie kneeled down beside him and looked at him.

'You look as though you've seen a ghost,' she said with a smile.

He conceded immediately. 'I just have.'

'What did you see?'

'A man, without a face, yet with a beard and an expression.'

'What expression?'

He thought about it a long time, remembering the apparition. 'It knew a great deal. It was wise, not surprised, pleased in a way that . . . I was doing what I was doing.'

'What were you doing?'

'Holding the crutch under my arm and using it . . . as a crutch.'

'You'll have to learn to separate the real thing from the fantasy.' She seemed concerned.

'What do you mean?'

'You didn't see anything that really existed, it was a projection of your mind, it was the guilt of not believing, of using the crutch, of all sorts of things manifesting themselves in your imagination.'

'Are you telling me I was hallucinating?'

'Possibly. Anxiety traces are quite distinctive, they are reproductions of what actually happened.'

'It was unnerving, whatever it was.'

'I don't believe in ghosts,' she said. 'There is absolutely no evidence that people can come back in any shape or form once they have died. What does happen, and very often, is that they leave something of themselves behind for others, like me, like you, to pick up.'

'So when you said 'Putain de béquille,' which loosely translated means 'whore of a crutch,' it was a reproduction of what Jaume Lanotte often said?'

'Yes. My whole theory of clairvoyance is based on traces.'

'What of precognition, seeing into the future as opposed to the past?'

'I think it's an intense build-up of a major manifestation to be. We all have precognition, we can all know what's going to happen to us. 'Intuition,' 'feelings', call it what you will. If hundreds of people feel strongly about something it can be made to happen. The religious call it 'praying'. A feeling is passed on and people like you can pick it up. We're certainly sending messages to each other, like you wanting to go to bed with me, which is the strongest vibration you send out. I pick it up, accept it or reject it.'

It was disarming. She was reading his mind.

'And I'm not a mind reader. I can't tell what you're thinking. I might be able to sometimes, but it's never certain. What I can do, like anyone else who sets their minds to work on their potential, is make a very good guess from expressions and from silences. Anyone who studies people can; palmists, psychiatrists, fortune tellers do this all the time.'

'Is there a range for these thought tranferences?'

'No. Telepathy can be practised across continents.'

'So what was I thinking about just then?'

'I don't know. I wasn't trying to find out. I wasn't switched on, as they say, correctly.'

'I have a very great desire to get away from here,' he said through a yawn. 'Do you think we could get on with the digging now?'

'If it's not too hot for you.'

'Where shall I start?'

'Where the crutch was lying before you moved it?'

He picked up the spade, flattened out the grass on the spot marked 'x' and dug into the hard, strong ground.

He hadn't done any digging for years; some people spent their whole lives with spades in their hands, he had hardly ever touched one.

'Do you want a hole going straight down, or do you want a grave?'

She was lying back with her head resting on her arms, watching him.

'Dig in a sort of circle, as though you were digging a deep hole, that way you might hit something.'

Though he wasn't going to admit it, he was quite enjoying the exercise. It was hard work, but healthy; sweat started coming down the side of his face; if he did more of this he might have a chance of losing some weight.

He was about a foot down now; the earth was softer, less stony, dark dank earth, nearly black, rich it seemed to him, when the spade hit something which snapped.

He uncovered it carefully and saw a grey bone, a chicken leg bone. He picked it up and held it up for Melanie to see.

She was dozing off, her eyes closed.

'Is this what you're looking for?'

She opened her eyes and immediately got up. She took the bone, examined it, then placed it against his shoulder.

'The clavicle. The collar bone,' she said. 'Where was it?'

He wasn't sure if she was joking.

'There,' he said pointing, and she got down on her knees and carefully dusted the earth away with her fingers, uncovering more bones.

'We'll have to be very careful now. It's archaeological work.'

'I think perhaps I'll leave it to you.'

'What we should do is dig all around the skeleton, then carefully move inwards.'

She took the spade from him and

marked off an approximate length.

'His head will probably be about here, his feet there,' she said, totally absorbed with the thought of the treasure to be revealed.

She didn't for a moment seem surprised that her intuition had been proved right.

He was stunned.

He took the spade from her and started digging a foot down on the area marked. Then the spade hit something again. He dusted it off and saw the unmistakable round shape of a skull.

'You're better at this than I am,' he said, leaning the spade against a tree and walking away from the site. 'I've just hit his head.'

Melanie bent down again and carefully picked the earth away from the exposed bone.

'He was buried face down,' she said over her shoulder.

Which is maybe why he was faceless, he thought. And the idea sent a shiver down his back. This extraordinary thing was actually happening!

From a dream of a battle to a wooden crutch in some remote farm in France, she had led him directly to the skeleton of a man who had been buried a hundred and fifty years ago. He wasn't sure which was more incredible, his inner need to disbelieve or what had now become reality.

He went back to Melanie, who was now scratching away at the earth with her nails and exposing the rest of the skeleton — the spine, the rib bones; there was cloth too, quite a lot, white, grey-green, brass buttons, no smell except that of the earth, no flesh or tissue. He watched as Melanie worked on.

'You'll ruin your hands,' he said.

'Where would the cross be, do you think?'

'Round his neck?'

'No. The chain was sent home. The cross was put in the grave with him. Just thrown in somewhere, maybe.'

He watched the patience with which Melanie worked, then went to the picnic bag, got himself a spoon and two knives and joined Melanie crouching over the grave. They must have looked like ghouls, or vultures, or both.

He loosened the earth where he expected bones to be with the knife, then removed it with the spoon.

'Wouldn't it be quicker if we just dug up the whole body and then sifted through for the cross?'

'Not here,' she said suddenly, picking up the spade and raking the earth from the pelvis down. 'This isn't him.'

'How do you know?'

'Look!'

He looked. The skull, the chest cage, the backbone, the pelvis, the legs. Two legs.

'We're looking for a one-legged man. Jaume Lanotte, according to Pierrot's letter, lost his leg. Where did you see the apparition?'

He pointed to where the faceless man had stood.

'But you said . . . ghosts didn't . . .'

'I said it wasn't a ghost. That's all. But if you saw something there, *there* is a good place to look. I can't explain everything logically, Michael; if I did I'd be like everyone else — unaware, blocked and blind to unbelievable possibilities.'

'I hope the whole regiment wasn't buried with him,' he said jokingly, moving towards the spot, but Melanie had crouched down again over the skeleton and was removing the earth from around one of the hands. He joined her to see what she was doing.

'I have a picture,' she said, 'based on nothing but supposition . . . but imagine the scene . . . three of them, Jaume Lanotte, Pierrot and Barrault. Jaume is dead. Pierrot wants to give him a Christian burial, Barrault doesn't. Barrault is greedy, wants the gold cross, the chain. They fight and one kills the other.'

'That doesn't tally with Pierrot's letter.'

'He wouldn't write about a murder, would he?'

'So he lied, you mean?'

'Wouldn't you?'

She moved to the other hand.

'You see, this one is clenched.'

She picked at the finger bones and delicately pulled out a small gold cross. It was very nearly miraculous.

She blew on it, cleaned it and held it out flat in the palm of her hand.

'Maria Dolores's cross. See what you can get from it.'

'What do you mean?'

'Hold the cross in your hand, close your eyes and just tell me what you feel, what you see. The cross has been buried and untouched by anyone living since it was held by that man, and by the girl to whom it belonged. If you're a descendant of hers as I believe you are, you should get a very strong reading.'

Relunctantly he took the cross, held it tightly and closed his eyes.

'Sit down,' Melanie said, taking him by the arm and leading him gently to the car rug.

The gold cross felt as though it was getting cold, then quite unexpectedly very hot.

'What can you feel? What can you see?' Melanie's voice came from a hundred miles away.

'It's very barren countryside, mountains, a few trees, low trees, small white houses, a white village, water in man-made gulleys

174

streaming down the furrows, plants, vegetables, not so barren now. A eucalyptus grove down in a dip. The distance is barren, but where I am standing it is not. I am with five, six other women working in the fields picking grapes, eating grapes, on a slope. I am dressed in white, the others are in black. I am very beautiful. I know this. I am proud of it, I don't want to spoil my hands picking grapes. There is a sense of fear and two men are up on the hill looking out for the enemy. I am not afraid of the enemy like the others. The enemy are human beings like everyone else; besides, they have been beaten and only marauders are left. Then the men wave frantically and the women scream and run away beckoning me to follow. I start following them towards the cortijo, the low white house, but I am following them because it means I need no longer work and spoil my hands, not because I am afraid. Then I am surprised to see my aunt running back towards me and the men up on the hill running down as fast as they can, but they are far away, a good half-hour away because of the valley. Now I see why there is the confusion and the panic, now I see the enemy and they are not frightening at all. Three French soldiers in ragged uniforms, but handsome, even with their beards, one, using a stout branch as a crutch, only has one leg. The bandage round it and the end of his knotted trousers are black with blood and horrible. The two younger ones are waving their swords and smiling. The cripple shouts something at them, an order; he is obviously an officer and now the other two are coming up to me. They are not smiling any more but all are tense. I do not like the look in their eyes. One gets hold of my wrists and twists my arms and it hurts. Oh God! . . . They are tearing my white dress off . . . my beautiful dress . . . and one of them is feeling me and . . . the cripple, staring at me like a madman, is undoing his buttons. I am trying to get away but the two men have pinned me down to the ground now and . . . '

A terrifying scream pulled him out of it. He was sitting up, staring wildly at Melanie, sweat pouring down his forehead.

'What happened?' he asked.

'You screamed. You were being raped . . . the cripple must have . . . '

He closed his eyes. He was a woman.

'No, it wasn't that.' He could feel a pain between his legs, a deep sensation, which hurt a little, but it wasn't that which had made him scream.

'My aunt,' he said. 'The soldier was on me, was in me . . . I didn't mind . . . I didn't mind, then I saw my aunt behind him, above us holding a pitchfork with both hands like a huge dagger. I screamed because I thought the prongs would not only go through him but through me as well . . . oh God, the blood . . . '

He sat up but kept his eyes closed, not wanting to lose the picture.

'One of the French soldiers . . . has severed her arm with his sword. There are screams and wails, they're picking up the cripple now, carrying him off. Then one of them is turning back, one of the French soldiers is turning back coming towards me, he's going to kill me! He grabs hold of the chain round my neck, my cross . . . '

Michael flinched as a sudden pain cut

across the back of his neck.

'He's broken the chain, taken it, they're running towards the trees, they've dropped the cripple now, have seen the men from the hill coming up the slope. I am sitting up trying to put my torn dress together, my cousins are coming towards me, the men from the hill are chasing the two Frenchmen. For a moment they stop, one hands the other my chain, my cross, then they part and start running in opposite directions, one much faster than the other. The men from the hill let him go and chase the other, they catch him. He screams like a rabbit, a screech, like a rabbit in a trap. It's over. I've got to my feet. I am standing up covering myself with a shawl. My aunt is being carried away. She is not dead but is bleeding badly. Now Antonio my brother is coming towards me. I am frightened of him, more frightened of him than of the French cripple. I put my hands up to protect my face. Oh!'

Michael opened his eyes, shook his head.

'Your brother slapped you?' Melanie asked.

'I disgraced the family,' he heard himself say. Then he came out of it, came out of the dream, the memory, the re-living of it all.

'They buried the cripple and the other in the eucalyptus grove. The third got away. The third must have been Pierrot.'

He took a deep breath and got to his feet. He could still feel the softness of the white dress against his legs, and instinctively felt round his neck for the cross.

'She was a very vain young woman, our Maria Dolores,' he said to Melanie. 'Her dress and the cross and the beauty of her hands were more important than anything else. I wanted the cross back,' he said, realizing he was still within Maria Dolores's personality, 'but they wouldn't take it from the soldier. So he was buried holding it.'

Melanie was sitting cross-legged on the car rug, the cassette recorder in front of her. She switched it off. He hadn't noticed her using it.

It had got dark now, the sky was mauve, the first stars were twinkling and he wanted to go. He had been a woman, as in his recurring dream with the man on the wall, he had been a woman.

'What have we learned?' he asked.

'Nothing definite. Jaume Lanotte forced himself on Maria Dolores. One must presume that the child from that union, from that rape, was Immaculada Almargo. But presumption isn't enough.'

'A rape and a murder, what more do you want? Wouldn't that sort of story, if it were true, become a legend in an area like this, in such a small pueblo?'

'Very likely,' Melanie said pensively. 'Let's go and ask a few questions.'

She started collecting together the crutch, the cassette recorder and the picnic bag, and folded the rug.

'What do I do with the cross?' Michael asked.

'Keep it. It's yours by inheritance.'

'What about the skeleton? We can't leave it like that.'

'No. Best cover it up.'

And with the spade he reinterred the remains of his forefather's friend.

★ ★ ★

The little pueblo changed completely at night.

Outside the small bar, folding chairs and tables had been put out and old men were sitting there sipping wine. There was noise, women in the streets, children playing in the dim light of the electric bulbs hanging from the wires slung across the roadways from one house to another.

The owner of the bar who had probably been working out in the fields all day was genial and seemed a good deal younger than his disagreeable wife. He wore a sweaty grey shirt, dirty trousers and a straw hat. His gums had receded leaving his yellow teeth nearly totally exposed, but he was talkative. In slow deliberate Spanish, he asked them what they were doing, and Michael was able to get the gist of what was being said, Melanie having learned the basics of the language in the States.

She lied, telling the publican they were archaeologists looking for Roman remains near the cemetery.

'Non!' he said emphatically. 'No son

Romanos, son Franceses de la guerra de Napoleon!'

'Si?' Melanie brightened up.

'Ahi esta el sitio de la Massacre de Maria Dolores.'

'A massacre?'

And as he poured them all out a good measure of wine, the men got closer to listen to the legend they had heard many times, but which made it no less enjoyable for all that.

The story was dissimilar to what he had relived only in the numbers. A regiment had come to Huejelar and taken *all* the women out into the fields and done those things to them which every soldier does to women. A young girl, Maria Dolores, however, cleverly enticed the soldiers into the eucalyptus grove where they were slaughtered by the men of the village.

'What happened to Maria Dolores?'

'She married a man from Nerja on the coast, but l'Abuelita's mother knew her. She knew her well!' Melanie translated for Michael when the bar owner had finished answering her question.

The Abuelita, Melanie then explained,

was the oldest woman in the village, a hundred and three years old, and she could be visited right now if they were really interested.

The whole village seemed to follow them to the low-roofed cortijo, where they found an old crone straight out of a medieval fairy tale, sitting fast asleep on a hard-backed chair.

The man from the bar gripped her shoulder and shook her.

'Estrangeros quieren conocer l'historia de Maria Dolores.'

'Maria Dolores?' She looked up, blinked, creased her face and waved her hand dismissing everyone.

'Maria Dolores es muerta.'

'She thinks we want to meet her,' Melanie said.

'Claro qu'ella es muerta, pero donde?' the bar man said.

'En Nerja. En Nerja en el cemeterio hombre.' And she closed her eyes and shut up like a clam. The audience was over.

The man from the bar, deeply apologetic, hunched his shoulders by way of explaining that he could do nothing about it, then ushered them out. But as Michael turned to have one last look at the centenarian, she opened one eye.

'Antes de morirse ella tiene cinco hijos y tres hijas.'

She held out her clenched fists apparently thinking she was showing the numbers of sons and daughters Maria Dolores had had, but arthritis had stopped her fingers from functioning.

'Y la primera hija no es Andaluz, es una bastarda francesa. Maria Dolores nunca era virgen!' she cackled, then closed up again.

'Did you understand that?' Melanie said. 'Eight children, the first one of which was obviously a French bastard.'

The eyes opened again, this time wider, and looked straight at Melanie. There seemed to be a complete understanding of what Melanie was, what she wanted and why.

'Su hija se casa con un Ingles. Ahora tu sabes todo.'

'What did she say?' Michael asked.

'The girl married an Englishman, and

now I know everything.'

Then the old woman turned to him and stretched out a long fingernail.

'Cuidado, hombre, esta mujer es peligrosa para ti.'

She smiled a knowing and now sinister smile, and closed her eyes.

'I didn't understand that,' he said.

'She just said that I was dangerous for you.'

And Michael interpreted the warning as the promise of a relationship he realized might be pleasantly inevitable.

8

Michael came to terms with himself and accepted the fact that Melanie was uncannily psychic and that he himself had strange powers of clairvoyance following two incidents, one unsettling, the other fearful.

Returning home after the Huejelar discoveries, they had cleared one of the guest rooms and transformed it into what amounted to an operations room, reproducing the family chart in large black letters on one of the white walls.

Everything connected up now except for Jeanne Chapelet, born in Melun 1567, and Marie Chapelet de Nostre-damme, born in Paris, 1594. The missing link could be provided by Sarah's and his own cannibalistic memories which, with medieval persons dying of hunger and eating their own children, suggested a siege in that period.

Melanie's researches had come up with

a number of likely sieges: Calais 1558, Chartres 1568, Rochelle 1573, Tournai 1581, Rouen 1591, Paris 1594, and one way of finding out which one was relevant was to go to each site and see if anything happened.

They had succeeded in Spain. Why not again?

They set off once more in the car with the intention of visiting each and every one of these sites, starting with Tournai castle in the South-West, then driving straight up to Chartres where they patiently tried to get a feeling of anxiety traces in the cathedral, but the experiment proved negative.

In the country hotel where they stayed that night, Michael awoke in a cold sweat hearing the distant sound of pneumatic drills, just as he had in Albacota. It was a strong enough experience for him to go into the next room and wake up Melanie.

'I've been hearing pneumatic drills and bulldozers,' he explained. 'I was wondering if you had?'

She immediately taped his description of what he'd heard and felt; he then took a tranquillizer and went back to bed, and slept heavily.

When they went down to breakfast the following morning, Michael saw a headline on the front page of someone's newspaper.

NEW SPANISH HOTEL COLLAPSES. 200 FEARED DEAD.

They went out to buy the paper and read the details of how the Claveles Hotel in Albacota had collapsed following a minor earth tremor.

There were photographs and eye-witness accounts of the disaster which occurred at four in the morning, and Michael realized that he'd seen it all three weeks before it had actually happened.

Over a strong black coffee he told Melanie how he had walked the streets of Albacota the night they had stayed there and seen the new hotel in ruins. Though she sympathised with what he was going through, the realization that it had been a premonition, that he might have saved people's lives if he had talked of it sooner,

188

made her angry at his stubborn determination to deny his own capabilities.

'Norma's died, Sarah's died, her husband died, all this was predicted by Sarah, your own daughter; you yourself have had the same dreams as her, the same premonitions, you have now foreseen a major disaster, yet you still don't believe enough to be open about it? How can you not believe? You have clairvoyant powers few others on earth have developed. You must use them!'

'To what end?' he asked.

'To prove to the disbelieving masses that our minds are much more than temporary banks for useless memories. Clairvoyance, remote viewing, precognition are early signs that the mind can manipulate, even destroy, physical and biological objects. Right now secret researches are being made in special laboratories set up by military and intelligence agencies because the psychic war will soon be on! I want to be armed and well armed before anyone else, and together we could have an overwhelming influence on the world.'

He said absolutely nothing, trying to take in Melanie's rather sudden and surprising outburst.

'A psychic war will soon be on?' he repeated.

'No one is taking any notice yet, but now and again some very versatile minds seem to do extraordinary things, don't you think? Only the ones who want glory come out in the open. Have you ever thought about those who never reveal themselves, like myself for instance? Nobody but you knows what I'm capable of, and even you don't know everything.'

It was the look in her eyes that was unsettling. For a moment he felt that perhaps he was in the presence of a fanatic.

★ ★ ★

In Paris they stayed at the St Germain Hotel where Michael had often stayed before.

Melanie did not insist on starting work straight away, rather the contrary; she was keen to be the simple tourist, admitting that she had never been to the top of the Eiffel Tower before and was curious to see the new Pompidou Centre.

He took advantage of this mood to take her to two of his favourite restaurants, one in the Etoile district for lunch, the other near the Porte St Denis for dinner.

It was really quite by chance, when they were walking towards the Rue La Fayette looking for a taxi, that he saw a very thin dog, limping, which sent a shiver down his back. It was a familiar dog, a grey, sickly mangy thing with yellow eyes, its rib cage sticking out, its tail recently torn off, blood red and wet as it tried to wag it on seeing him.

'What are you looking at?' Melanie asked as the dog passed them.

'That dog.'

'What dog?'

He stopped and looked back for the dog but it had disappeared.

'A yellow dog, very thin, mangy with no tail, Pollux, belonged to the apothecary . . . ' He froze. The words had come out so naturally, it was uncanny.

He closed his eyes. He had slipped

back into the past so easily. He then forced himself to think of the dog again and remembered seeing it lift its skinny leg at the corner of a building, all wood with overhanging beams, cobble stones, steps leading down to the left. He was there now with that agony of hunger, though he had just eaten a four-course meal. He opened his eyes.

'It was down here on the left, a small street leading to a market place with the church where they set up the communal kitchen.' He led the way, taking Melanie's hand and looking up and around at the modern blocks. He was going to get lost, the past had been buried and built over, then looking at the ground he noticed the corner stone of an older building.

'That was there. That's old. Original. The street went down here.'

There was no street, just a solid wall rising some eight storeys above them.

'It's in there somewhere, they've built this on the site. Let's go round it.'

They circumnavigated the whole block which covered a large area. To get inside they would have to wait till the morning, for the two huge sets of doors leading into the courtyard were closed and locked for the night and they could hardly wake up the concierge with the request that they were looking for a sixteenth-century siege.

He sketched the area roughly on a piece of paper and marked the place where he had seen the dog and recognized the corner stone. Then they went back to the hotel.

★   ★   ★

Michael was awake at six thirty and went to knock on Melanie's door. She was already dressed.

'I was going to wake you up at seven,' she said.

'How did you digest the crab soufflé?'

'Marvellously. I slept like a log.'

He squeezed her arm. He had had little difficulty in persuading her to try something new, she was becoming a gourmet.

He went back to his room, washed and shaved and got dressed, admitting that he was excited at the prospect of the morning's work. He enjoyed the research, the detection. He had slept well, without a tranquillizer, and had had no dreams or nightmares.

Rue St Agnieul was different during the day. There was a market nearby and people were setting up stalls; the butchers and greengrocers were opening, lorries were unloading and there were packing cases everywhere. Clear, clean water ran down the gutters and the smell of fresh coffee was in the air.

They found the corner stone easily enough and the huge entrance doors farther on were now open. Melanie checked that her cassette recorder, hanging from a shoulder strap, was ready to be switched on.

Through the doors a short tarmac drive-in led to an inner courtyard with trees and a gravel path winding its way round various flower beds to apartment and office entrances. The concierge was not yet up; her door was closed and the curtains drawn, so they had a chance to have a good look round, but there was nothing at all to remind Michael of anything in particular.

They decided to leave and go round the block as they had the night before. In London there would have been a mews perhaps, but here there seemed to be no other way in.

They walked around three sides of the building, then unexpectedly they came upon a spiked gate which obviously opened into a narrow alley between two buildings. Michael had no recollections, no feelings, but it was such an obvious place to go down that they tried the door. It was locked. The street they were in was completely deserted and while Melanie kept a look-out, Michael grabbed hold of the spikes and pulled himself up to see over the top.

The alley was dark, cobbled, about twenty-five feet in length and led to a door in the side of a very old building, a church. He knew the church, he knew the crypt door, and now he remembered that it had all happened in the crypt.

'How on earth do we get in there?'

'Ask around, I suppose,' Melanie suggested.

'What excuse do we give?'

Melanie smiled, held up her canvas hold-all and suddenly threw it over the spiked door.

'What did you do that for?' Michael asked, aghast.

'Last night we were chased by a couple of muggers, we got away by throwing the bag over the top. Now we want to get it back.'

'Muggers? This isn't New York.'

'Oh, come on! Paris is wonderful but crimes are committed here as well, you know.'

It was a good idea, and gave them the excuse they wanted. They started asking around. Sympathy, indifference — they met every trait in human nature, but no one had the key.

Eventually a concierge down the road helped them most; the place belonged to a convent which had moved to the country years ago and the crypt was used for storing their furniture. Best thing was to climb over the top.

Michael borrowed a couple of packing cases from a market stall round the corner, stacked them up and was able to get high enough to ease himself up and over, though at one moment the spikes came dangerously near to ripping his trouser leg.

Melanie, agile as a cat, followed him, the excuse being, if anyone asked, that an earring had also been lost and four eyes to search for it were better than two.

Once they were both over they found themselves trapped in the dark, dank, cobbled passage, the noise of the outside world completely cut off. Together they walked up to the crypt door.

The iron handle turned easily enough and although the door wasn't locked, the door and the jamb were secured by a small padlock. It was so ridiculously small compared to the door and so obviously easy to break if they had had a crowbar that it was irritating. Access was barred to them by a very small piece of metal and there was nothing they could do about it.

To Michael's annoyance Melanie just stood quite still and stared at the problem. Her very composure was aggravating. She had so often dealt successfully with such problems that he had come to rely on her to solve things, but he didn't see how she would deal with this one.

'I want you to do something for me,' she said, very quietly.

'Mm?'

'I want you to go to the other end of the passage and face the door and not turn round till I say.'

He was about to ask why, but she held up her hand. 'And please don't ask any questions.'

Then, assuming Melanie wished to obey the call of nature, he smiled, turned round and went to the other end of the passage. Keeping his eyes on the door he started counting. He hadn't done this since last playing hide-and-seek, which must have been years ago. When he reached a hundred he expected her to call out, but she said nothing.

He didn't want to embarrass her so he went on counting but when he got to two hundred he decided that that was enough and sneaked a look. To his surprise Melanie was not there and the door was wide open.

He ran down the passage, looked at the padlock which was miraculously open, and went inside the crypt.

It was pitch dark.

'Melanie?'

'Yes, I'm here.'

'How did you get in?'

'The simple use of a hairpin.'

'Why didn't you want me to watch?'

'It makes me nervous and anyway I made a solemn promise to the person who taught me how to do it never to show anyone else.'

His eyes were getting accustomed to the dark now and he noticed a small barred window up to his right.

'Close the door,' Melanie said, 'then we can get used to the dark completely. There are some beautiful pieces in here. Look at that lectern, and this altar piece.'

Michael closed the door and was instantly aware of a too-familiar smell. It was terribly sickly, a wet smell, not of burning but of over-boiled, over-stewed fish, meat, rotting vegetables, the nauseous smell of putrefaction.

'Is it here?' he heard Melanie's voice

ask from somewhere far away. He tried to answer but found he couldn't; his throat was dry and he found it hard to breathe. He realized he was itching all over and had to scratch his bony arms.

He looked up at the barred window and saw it gradually get larger. It was quite extraordinary; it got longer as he watched, as though it were made of some soft plastic, or was melting. It was changing shape, and then it became obscured by the steam from the cauldron just below it where Melanie was standing, still as a rock, mesmerized by what was taking place around them.

The wailing sent a shiver down his back, the heavy breathing behind him and the gangrenous smell of the man who brushed past him, cheeks sunk into the hollows of his mouth, eyeballs protruding beyond the sockets.

People now appeared from the shadows, all deathly pale, moving slowly as though every effort was costing them their lives.

Suddenly Melanie screamed.

It was sheer terror in her voice and he

saw her surrounded by three of the ghostly figures who were trying to grab hold of her but were too weak. They were caressing her arms, her legs, feeling her body, their eyes greedy with hunger. He extended his own arm and saw it was just grey skin and bone.

A woman passed by holding the child from the memory, a thin baby, lifeless yet still breathing. She stripped it of the little clothing it had and dropped it head first into the cauldron. The man with the stick stirred it and then the door at the far end, the double doors of the crypt entrance, suddenly opened and four scraggy individuals burst in pulling behind them a mat of woven reeds on which was the body of a fat man. Instantly the horde crowded around him and picked off his clothes and dismembered him like carrion on a dead antelope.

'Stop them!' Melanie screamed in terror. 'Stop them!'

She was digging into herself, tearing at her own shoulders, drawing blood at the hideousness of it all. The woman who had thrown the child in the vat danced by, holding an arm dripping blood from its wrenched shoulder, her eyes staring, her mouth in the shape of a grin.

He turned to look at what was happening to the corpse. The stronger of the men who had dragged it in was twisting the head round and round, brutally twisting it till the bones cracked, and while the others held the remains of the trunk he pulled, and someone hacked with a knife, and like a clod of grass which is being uprooted, it suddenly came away.

He shut his eyes tight, then felt an ice-cold grip on both his wrists. He looked up, wildly, there were several of them grabbing him by the throat, the arms, the ankles, they were lifting him and were going to put him straight into the boiling water. He screamed. His mouth was forced open and a stick introduced between his teeth. This was it. This was how it was going to end.

They dragged him towards the cauldron, then for some reason away from it towards the small door, and he saw his own hand, his own wrist with the blue cuff, his watch, he blinked and looked at the people holding him and realized they were healthy, concerned people dressed in everyday clothes. He saw Melanie, her finger to her lips anxiously looking on, begging silence.

'Allez mon vieu, tranquille. Tranquille, on va pas te faire mal . . . '

They laid him down on a pew, someone somewhere found a light switch and several dim bulbs went on in the vaulted ceiling. Four people were standing around him, an elderly woman in a black dress was holding out a glass of water. Melanie, sitting opposite him on a chair, her hair wet, perspiring, was drinking water from another glass.

'What happened?' he asked. He was now aware that he was out of breath.

'You're an epileptic and have had a fit. Just go along with that. We'll talk later,' Melanie said quickly.

'Did you see it all?' he asked her.

'Yes. Yes, I saw it. Don't talk now.'

Outside he heard a police siren, and shortly after two men in uniforms arrived with a stretcher.

Chatter in whispers, suggestions, advice, then the efficient men pushing everyone aside, looking at him, examining his eyes, lifting his eyelids, taking his pulse, asking him to stand, to walk, taking Melanie's pulse.

They threw a blanket over him and a blanket over her and led them quietly, gently, out of the horror crypt into the passage and into broad daylight. A large crowd had gathered in the street. The police were there holding them back.

'Qu'est ce qui se passe? Quoi? Pour-quoi? Qui es?'

For tragedies people took time off.

They entered the comparative comfort of the ambulance — tinted windows, people staring in, not seeing. He sat down and closed his eyes; the smell was still in his nostrils; how could something of the past, of hundreds of years ago, still be so pungent, so sickening? Those hands, his hands, that wretched dried skin, the sores.

The ambulance moved off with its fanfare alarm echoing and re-echoing, clearing the streets ahead. How shattering for those who had experienced an accident, yet how comforting for him, the sound of modern security.

'Did you hear what I said, Michael?' he heard Melanie ask. 'You had an epileptic fit. We were in there looking for my handbag and you had a fit.'

He nodded. He couldn't speak, couldn't quite separate the past from the present. What had made them materialise? Those awful beings. His own powers? Melanie's? Had they intruded on a world that went on recurring? Did they go on living in there, those anxiety traces?

Then, unexpectedly, he vomited, so quickly he couldn't control it. The male nurse was ready for him, a plastic bowl was there, a towel, orders were given to slow down. It wasn't nausea, it was the sickness of four centuries, the taste in his mouth of that white flesh, the bone fished out of the vat and picked clean white. What did they do with the heads, the eyes?

And he retched.

He felt himself trembling, shaking all over. They'd think he was going into another fit. He saw the syringe, the nurse holding the needle up, the little jet of liquid to check, the smell of surgical spirit, his shirt sleeve up, the jab. He had to tell Melanie before he forgot, before he lost consciousness . . .

'The man who did the stirring, the old man, he and I were the only survivors . . . he was the father of my child . . . and I died, didn't I? Like Sarah I died before ever seeing it . . . '

His head began to thunder, his eyes became blurred. It would be all right, this was what was wanted, the jab was working. And the last thought he had before he blacked out was a question . . .

How had they got in?

Melanie never used hairpins.

* * *

They kept Michael in hospital for two days, fed him well and checked up on all his possible physical defects as well as his identity papers.

They were very discreet and no charges were made against him for breaking and entering. Melanie handled the whole business with her usual calm. The story was quite simple. They had both been mugged the night before, she had thrown her handbag over the gate, they had climbed over to retrieve it and the effort, presumably, had brought on the fit. He had raved, had attacked the wrong door to get out, had somehow wrenched the lock open and had had the fit inside the crypt. She had screamed her head off and people had broken down the gate and come to her rescue. Most had hoped for a murder or rape; no one ever suspected that inside the crypt both had relived the horror of the St Denis siege.

One disadvantage resulting from the episode was that the police took away Michael's driving licence until he could come up with medical proof certifying that he was not subject to fits. He therefore laid up the car in a garage and booked Melanie and himself air tickets back to Nice.

The flight was comforting, and he decided that they should both have a rest, get away from it all. Melanie had been terrified, still was, had admitted to it, to having nightmares. Together they had experienced a supernatural horror and this, with the eucalyptus grove and for him the Albacota disaster, added up to strain on his nerves which would prove too much for him if he didn't put a stop to it. The comfort and security of being in a modern airliner with all its gadgets and its speed was helpful. He took her hand, and sipping a glass of cool orange juice, suggested going to New York for a break. He wanted to see a number of people on business. They could stay at the Eden Boulevard Hotel until they had both recovered.

Melanie agreed without arguing. They had achieved the incredible. He was a medium of no uncertain power and proving whether or not he was a descendant of Nostradamus was hardly relevant now. Clearly he was, clearly the memory he had relived was that of Jeanne Chapelet who had survived the siege by eating human flesh only to die in childbirth. Pierette Chapelet de Nostre-damme was her daughter; the dates and location recorded in documents fitted. It closed the family circle. What Michael should do now was project himself forward, not backward.

'Not if it means experiencing the aftermath of earthquakes before they happen.'

'But what if they were premonitions of delights? The knowledge that a pair of long legs were lonely in the next hotel room, or that a certain number was to come up at roulette?'

'You sound like a mediocre devil using a very old tempting device to acquire my beautiful soul. I have read and learnt from Dr. Faustus, thank you. What I would like to foresee, to begin with, is my own destiny.'

'Maybe that would be unwise.'

★ ★ ★

They stayed three days in Cagnes, then they took a flight directly to New York from Nice.

The usually tedious and exhausting business of airports and jet travel en masse was what he wanted most, the feeling of belonging to a group of live people engaged in a space-age activity. The three nights spent alone in his own bedroom had been anxious ones, fearing his memories, fearing premonitions.

Now he felt so relaxed and distant from the recent past that when he lay back and adjusted his seat belt he half-hoped he would slip into a dream, but something pleasant. And he did, quite easily.

He was instantly on a pier waving goodbye to a family leaving on a boat. Beside him two children his own age. He was a child for he was holding someone's hand, someone he trusted and loved, and he wore a sailor suit and a straw boater.

'Are you all right?' Melanie asked. 'You're breathing very deeply.'

She was looking after him, was concerned for his well being. He was valuable property now. He'd try and seduce her in New York, that would bring them both down to earth.

'I was on a quayside waving goodbye to someone. I was a boy of about six. Victorian, I should say.'

'Your grandfather?'

210

His grandfather. He was probably his own grandfather. Why not? He could be his own grandfather, mother, great grandfather on both sides, but never his uncle or aunt or sister or brother.

He shifted position, opened an eye to look at the white clouds below, the old familiar snow scene. He closed his eyes again.

The flash came vividly, and he sat up.

'What?' Melanie begged to know. 'What was it?'

'I was in the elevator at home, pressing the buttons, and nothing worked.'

'What else?'

'Nothing else.'

She shrugged her shoulders and settled back.

'It wasn't a prediction, it was a forewarning,' he said. 'Most disconcerting.'

He rang for the hostess and asked for a large whisky.

'Are you going to get drunk?'

'Why not, we're on holiday.' And he squeezed her leg in a most unfatherly way, and she raised her eyebrows but did not remove his hand. So he left it there and enjoyed the feeling of that young thigh under the pleated skirt.

When the drink came he had to let go to take the glass, but after taking a sip he returned his hand to where it had been, and she made no move to take it away.

Happy, he fell asleep.

* * *

In the window of the Shohlmann Gallery, West Broadway, was an oil painting by Raulk.

It was a landscape, either Italian or Spanish, quite different in style from the three Michael had at home.

He walked into the gallery and looked at the collection: all landscapes, Florence and environs in fact, pale pinks, pallid skies, autumn, winter, a period he had no idea Raulk had been through. He was impressed and pleased, it added value to his small collection.

'I have three of his later works,' he said to the gallery manager. 'Quite different to this.'

'He went through three different periods,' the man said. 'What date are yours?'

'Seventy-one, seventy-two . . . '

'Very valuable now. We're hoping to exhibit his last mountain landscapes, including the one he was working on when he died.'

'What?'

'He was killed two weeks ago. You didn't know? It was in all the papers. Most extraordinary circumstances, struck by lightning. They believe it was his easel, made of metal, which attracted the thunderbolt.'

Michael made some appropriate disbelieving noises of sympathy and hid his face by peering more closely at one of the oils. Then when he had recovered his composure a little he walked out.

Raulk dead.

Of all people.

He could have warned him.

But how?

Raulk would never have believed him. How would you warn a person without first convincing them that you were

213

psychic, that it was in your power to know the future? And people would want proof.

What of Sigrid?

He would ring her immediately, try to contact her, find out more.

So many people around him dying.

When would the phase end, the cycle, if it was a cycle?

He walked down Fifth Avenue and decided to buy Melanie a present. He had never given her anything, yet they had become very close, and now, with this latest news, he realized she was his only friend. Whom else did he have on earth who knew so much about him, whom he could trust?

He stopped outside a boutique selling antique jade. He went in. A necklace with earrings to match? Did she wear earrings? Were her ears pierced? He bought the set and went back to the hotel.

Melanie was lying on her bed reading the newspaper. She seemed quite content so he said nothing about Raulk.

He handed her the leather presentation case. She looked at him as if unsure whether she should accept it.

Then she opened it and her eyes widened.

'Did you know this was my stone and my favourite colour?'

He hadn't known.

Or had he?

Perhaps he knew everything without being aware of it.

She gave him a peck on the cheek.

'Why?' she asked.

'Because I think you deserve it, and I can afford it.' He then told her about Raulk, but she hardly reacted. His life would be full of such premonitions; the trick was to recognize them and make use of them.

They had lunch in a restaurant he knew. She felt more at home in New York, she enjoyed the pallid food more, shook on the sauces, the spices, was able to drink Coca Cola without feeling embarrassed. Why not, if that's what she really enjoyed? She was a high-school kid still. Hamburgers. Memories of childhood. He watched her eat a large ice-cream sundae as artificial as the glass was tall. She sucked the Coke through a straw. She was really very young.

She enjoyed those hamburgers at lunch so much that he treated her to more early in the evening as they contemplated going to a movie. They had a couple of drinks, became aware that they were enjoying each other's company, so much so that she suggested going back to the hotel.

In the elevator, alone for the first time that evening, he kissed her on the mouth, and she responded. He'd so neatly placed the thought of going to bed with her to the back of his mind that being suddenly aroused like this unsettled him.

'Now look young lady, this sort of behaviour leads to rape.'

'It doesn't have to.'

'With me it does. I'm a descendant of Jaume Lanotte, remember.'

'I mean it doesn't have to be rape.'

The elevator stopped at their floor and they got out. She found his hand which held the keys to their separate rooms, took his key and put it in his jacket pocket.

'You won't need that one tonight.'

216

She let him open her door and led the way in.

It was dark, the time getting on for nine o'clock.

'Do you mind if we keep the lights off, this first time?' she asked.

He pinned her against the wall and embraced her melodramatically. Melanie laughed, he undressed her slowly, then carried her to the bed.

As he took off his own clothes, getting used to the semidarkness, he noticed that she had moved a mirror and leaned it against a table so that she could see herself from her bed. Maybe now he'd find out what that fantasy was all about.

He got into the bed beside her and she was on him like a leech, trembling, feverishly passionate; he had to struggle to get his breath.

It was quick. Far too quick. She murmured and sighed and he didn't know whether she was pretending or not. At his age he should have had more control, but he was like a teenager, unable to check the too-sudden excitement.

'I'm sorry,' he said.

'Why?'

'Un poco rapido!'

'It was nice. It was me giving and you taking, and that's what I wanted.'

Was she on the Pill, this naive child?

'Are you on the Pill?'

'I'm on all sorts of things,' she said crawling over him again. 'Do you think you can manage it twice?'

She was sliding on him, very light, kissing him. She was no virgin, she never had been. He had been deceived all the time, had wanted to believe her innocent. He was the naive child. She got off him suddenly, lay on her back on the edge of the bed and reached out for the light switch.

He thought of the mirror. Was it performance time now, then?

'I'm going to the bathroom,' she said, and got up. She walked naked across the room, leaving the door open so that he could hear what was going on. How could such a shy girl suddenly become so brazen?

She reappeared and posed in the doorway, then got in the bed beside him again. She grabbed hold of him and started to excite him, she moved over him and he played possum, then when he was roused turned her over and was on her.

For a moment there was a struggle, an imitation struggle with imitation protests, but he was in her and he thrust, again and again, confident now, knowing he would last, delighted he could last, and she moved with him for a long time and then suddenly she lay quite still and he felt himself being drawn, sucked in by a quite incredible force.

It was liquid, tactile, an orgasm that came unexpectedly quickly yet went on, on and on, draining him endlessly. For a moment he imagined he was stuck to a vast woman with the energy of a gigantic animal. He held his breath, he could feel the sperm being pulled out of him. He tried to withdraw but he was gripped like a vice between her thighs which were vibrating. He pushed himself up from her but could not get out; it was as though he were caught by a centrifugal machine whirring him round and sucking his very being, his soul, his strength all out through this endless tube between his legs, this mile-long umbilical cord connecting him to the infinite.

He felt himself going faint, dizzy, then he was released. He came out, fell alongside her, felt her body lying there, totally relaxed, limp even. How could such a fragile girl have so much power? Is that what she had meant, having so much power between them? Was this one of the bonuses that came along with the gift of clairvoyance? He had never known anything like it.

'Are you all right?' he murmured through his exhaustion.

She didn't answer. She was breathing heavily, regularly, fast asleep.

He took some deep breaths himself. The sensation had been incredible. He would want to do that again and again. God, he would want to do that again.

Unbelievable.

Then the telephone rang.

He reached out for the receiver, irritated. Someone had the wrong number. Nobody knew he was there, unless it was for her.

The female voice at the other end was familiar and simply said 'Hallo.'

'Who is that?'

'It's me.'

'Who's me?' An ex-girl friend who had seen him in the hotel? Knew they had separate rooms? He knew the voice but couldn't place it.

'It's me, Melanie.'

'What do you mean, Melanie?'

'It's me, Melanie, the little redhead you've just laid.'

He glanced over his shoulder at Melanie, who was fast asleep. Was it a two-way mirror? Had someone in the next room been watching them?

'Who *is* that?'

'It's *me*, Michael, Melanie Forbes.'

He held onto the receiver, sat up and shook Melanie. Her body was quite cold. Ice cold.

He looked at her, the skin was so pale it was nearly transluscent.

'Astral projection, Michael. I'm not with you in bed, I'm back here in Cagnes, in your house.'

It was her voice. Some sort of

221

ventriloquist trick.

He shook the body next to him, looked at himself doing so in the mirror.

'Say something,' her voice asked.

'Who are you really?' He was frightened.

'This is Melanie, speaking to you from Cagnes, south of France,' the voice said slowly, patiently. 'I've left my physical body and am here.'

'What do you mean?'

'I've travelled through space, Michael. Astral projection. Did you enjoy what we just did?'

'Yes,' he said politely.

'We make a great team, don't we?'

He was recovering. It was some sort of joke. He didn't know how it was being played but she had got an accomplice or something and was pretending to be asleep next to him.

He had to admit the timing was perfect.

'Where exactly are you?' he asked.

'On the top floor in the penthouse drawing room, lying full length on the sofa.'

'How can you be lying full length on the sofa without a body?' He'd got her there.

'Mentally.'

He didn't say anything.

'You don't believe me, do you? Tell you what. Ring me back. Just put the receiver down and ring me back. You know the number, or should do. You can dial.'

The voice rang off.

He put the receiver down slowly, then slipped out of bed very quickly. Somehow Melanie's inert body next to him, cold, pale, made him uneasy.

Slowly he drew off the blanket, the top sheet, and stared at her. She was quite white.

He switched on the centre light. It was like looking at a marble sculpture.

He touched her. The flesh was hard and bloodless, the lips white, her eyes tight shut, the fists clenched. She was doubled up in a foetal position, as though cringing from an impact.

He slipped his hands under her and turned her over. There were bruises on her shoulders, bruises and scratches down her back, not sex scratches; it was as though she had been through a hailstorm, or a triplex window.

'Melanie?' he said in a loud whisper.

Nothing.

He threaded his hand between her arms to get to her wrist, to feel her pulse. The rate was incredibly slow, fifteen, sixteen beats to the minute.

He reached out for the telephone and started dialling his Cagnes number, then put the receiver down. He picked it up again and called the operator instead and asked for the number.

'You can dial it, caller.'

'I know. But I'd like you to get it for me, please, I have . . . an injury.'

'Oh, I'm sorry, caller. I'll get it straight away.'

He put the receiver down again. What kind of injury would stop a man dialling?

Her problem, not his.

He put his hand on Melanie's thigh. Then he stroked her hair. It was brittle, wet.

The 'phone rang.

'I'm putting you through, caller. The

number is ringing.'

It rang four times, then someone picked up the receiver at the other end.

'Hi!' Melanie's voice said.

'Just explain to me how you do it.'

'You believe me, then?'

'Yes, I believe you.' He was going to keep calm, go along with it.

'You should believe it. I've done it before. Remember the time you found the elevator repairmen in the house and Sarah's dressing gown in your room . . . ?'

He remembered.

'That was one of my first try-outs. Then when you found me nude in Renoir's garden, that wasn't too success-ful. I just got as far as the beach where luckily I wasn't noticed because they swim nude there.'

She giggled. To her it was a game.

'How do you do it?' He asked.

'Mind over matter,' she said simply. 'Anyone can do it if they work on themselves. I'm going to come back now. You can watch if you want to, but it might put you off me. I understand one goes into spasms and jerks rather a lot. See ya!'

And she rang off.

He was cold. He got up and went to put on his bathrobe. He then switched on all the lights in the room, made sure the door was locked, took a chair and placed it near the bed and sat down, never for one moment taking his eyes off her.

Nothing happened for quite a while.

He got up, put on his wrist watch. Twenty-eight minutes past nine.

Maybe she was dead.

Then he saw a muscle in her arm twitch, like the nerve of a spider's dismembered leg.

Her arms unfolded as though the liquid of life was flowing back into her. Her head moved, then both her legs slowly stretched out.

She rolled over on her back, her fingers extended and she uncoiled until she was quite rigid in a spreadeagle position. Her whole being then started to vibrate as though an electric current were going through her. Then she sat bolt upright, opened her eyes and he gasped.

She had no eyes.

They were just white.

The head turned, the white eyes stared straight at him unseeing, her whole frame then went into an extreme convulsion and, as though an outer force was taking hold of her and shaking her, she was violently picked up and thrown across the room, hit the wall by the door and fell into a dead faint.

He didn't move.

She was breathing very heavily now, more and more rapidly. She opened her eyes again; this time they were normal. She was sweating, soaking, she mopped her brow, kneeled down, rubbed her bruises and looked up.

'God, I don't want to do that again,' she said, and started getting up.

'Can you help me? I'm really badly hurt.'

He helped her to the bed and she lay down, then she sat up and, as though gripped by a high voltage current, stiffened, gasped, and all the lights went out.

In the darkness he stumbled about looking for his lighter. Opening the door he realized there was confusion at the elevator gates, someone was calling out but being told not to panic, help was at hand.

Holding the lighter over Melanie he now found her lying back on the bed her eyes closed, breathing normally. Looking out of the window he saw that the whole of the city was pitch black; only the faint glow from across the Hudson told him that the disaster was restricted.

He knew he should leave Melanie to rest but he wanted to know what had happened. The coincidence of her throwing a fit at the same time as the blackout might be explained by her being affected by whatever had caused the failure, but he was learning fast that coincidences were too easy an explanation for things he did not understand, did not want to accept.

He touched her arm, she was warm.

She moved slightly, murmured something he couldn't make out. He put his hand on her forehead, it was damp, but not particularly hot.

'Melanie?' he said in the darkness.

'Hallo.'

'Are you all right?'

'Sure. It wasn't me alone. I couldn't have done it alone.'

'What?' He was very confused.

'Could I have a glass of water? I'm terribly thirsty. Best fill up the basin and the bath. There's going to be a shortage.'

He found his way to the bathroom, plugged in the bath and the washbasin, turned on the cold taps, filled up a glass and went back to give it to Melanie.

'There's a flashlight in my zip-bag,' Melanie said. 'I brought it in case of emergencies.'

He found it, switched it on, put it on a table facing the mirror so it would throw out more light, then he heard the water flow running down. Everyone had had the same idea.

He watched Melanie drink the water. She handed him the empty glass, lay back on the pillow and was instantly asleep like an exhausted child after a day on the beach.

He went back to the bathroom, turned off the taps and closed the door. In the dark he took off his bathrobe and sat

229

down on the lavatory. The numbness he had felt in his stomach now turned to colic. He had been afraid. For the last hour or so he had suppressed the feeling of fear, but he had been afraid. His stomach had twitched and contracted and now it was all sickness and the feeling that it wasn't over. He was no longer dealing with a normal human being. Memory, even predictive faculties, could be explained, but this last demonstration was something he knew he couldn't handle. Melanie wasn't just dabbling in psychic research, she was more advanced than that; she was playing with occult powers and that was dangerous.

Somehow he would have to stop her.

9

Every newspaper in the world carried the story.

The great New York blackout.
New York total power failure.
The night civilization switched off.

It made headlines everywhere. Stories abounded about looting in the streets, shortage of water, people getting stuck in elevators, the surprise of the telephones working, ice melting, food rotting, hospitals straining their generator systems, enterprising young men selling iced beer from New Jersey for five times the price; the city came to a complete standstill for twenty-five hours.

Consolidated Edison, the New York power utility explained the phenomenon. Three lightning bolts had struck five high-voltage overhead power lines, first knocking out two thousand nine hundred megawatts from upstate, then two thousand megawatts from another source. The automatic cutoffs had gone into action to protect the system from permanent damage, and the lights of New York City went out.

Melanie did not wake up till lunchtime the following afternoon.

New York was now totally paralyzed by the power failure and sweating it out in the sweltering heat. The full reliance on electricity was making itself felt, the natural taken-for-granted activities of the city dweller appeared to be ninety-five per cent manufactured. No communication, no transport, no water and no way of getting cool.

Michael did not leave the hotel room. Having been woken up at nine o'clock for a milk and cornflakes breakfast, with apologies from the management, he realized that it wasn't going to be the breakaway holiday he had envisaged.

During the morning he had noticed Melanie shivering; he had covered her up with blankets and watched over her as though she were a sick child.

When she eventually stirred and awoke, she sat up, stretched herself, rubbed her eyes and smiled at him as though nothing in the world had happened.

'How are you feeling?' he asked.

'Fine. A little bruised.'

'You remember what happened?'

'Of course I remember,' she said with a laugh.

'It was good, wasn't it?'

'Us, you mean?' he asked, uncertain.

'Us! Our sexual intercourse. Did you enjoy it?'

'Yes. Very much.' He didn't like discussing it. A French girl he'd once been to bed with had spent the whole of the next day analyzing his technique and that had been terrible. Was Melanie another one of those?

'Would you like to do it again?'

'Of course.'

'Now, I mean.'

'Aren't you tired?'

'Are you? There's nothing else to do, they won't get the trouble fixed for a few hours. But I'd like something to eat first, and a little champagne perhaps?'

He ordered lunch, cold meat salad, cheese, canned fruit cocktail, a bottle of champagne. They apologized but could not bring it up to the fifteenth floor, could they come down to the dining room?

Melanie got dressed and they went down to the restaurant, ate by candlelight in the hot, unconditioned atmosphere. Then they climbed back up to their room, slowly, carrying champagne glasses and two more bottles.

She refused to discuss the night's events and made no reference to her remark, 'I couldn't have done it alone.' He didn't press. He'd find out sooner or later.

They went to bed.

It was nothing like the night before, pleasant, but not exceptional. They went to sleep in each other's arms and when they awoke six hours later the electricity had been restored.

They had a late snack in the Village during which Melanie suggested hiring a car, getting out of New York, and going to visit her old home.

'It's in the wilds of Virginia, an old farmstead.'

★　★　★

On the way to Clifton Forge via Washington and Richmond in a bright blue Pontiac, Melanie talked of her background, something she had never really talked about before.

Her mother had married a young farmer named Herbert Forbes who had two aunts who had been mediums, dead now.

' . . . Which is maybe why I'm a bit psychic.'

A bit!

He had to admit that for the last two travelling days he had managed to forget what had happened in New York. Melanie had slept peacefully and shown no signs of going into trances on their first night in a motel, and she hadn't once read his mind. He hadn't had a dream, or a memory, or sensed a prediction, maybe she had exhausted both their resources.

Melanie's family home was a disappointment. There was no one left, the farmstead was owned by someone else, developed into a poor holiday camp which was closed. She didn't really remember it, it had just been somewhere to go.

She apologized for taking him all the way there for nothing, but he genuinely didn't mind. He had got away from all the fear for more than forty-eight hours, which was an achievement in itself.

In a motel outside Lynchburg that night, however, it started again.

'I've got news for you,' Melanie said, getting into bed.

'You have?'

'You're going to be a daddy.'

He laughed — a little nervously, but he laughed.

'A little bit too soon to know, don't you think?'

'No. I know. It'll be a boy and it'll be the most powerful child ever. Can you imagine? A boy fathered by a direct descendant of Nostradamus whose mother is one of the famous Forbes family is destined to be pretty magnificent, don't you think?'

'The *famous* Forbes family?'

Melanie got out of bed, opened her zip-bag and brought out a thick paperback volume. *A Directory of the Occult.*

She got back into bed, flicked over the pages and handed it to him open. Under *Spiritualism. Its History:* he read:

FORBES A completely new epoch in the history of occultism opened on the evening of 5th March 1846 in the house of the Forbes family in the township of Clifton Forge, Virginia, U.S.A. For some time the family had been disturbed by rapping noises and on that evening the two Forbes girls, aged 14 and 16, asked the mysterious knocker to repeat the noises. The spirit did so. It was then discovered the Forbes sisters seemed to provoke rapping noises wherever they went . . .

'They're your what?'

'They were my grandfather's aunts, my great-great-aunts. So you see, our union is bound to produce a fairly remarkable child.'

'Melanie,' he said as calmly as he could, 'I think you're going over the top. After a few days you can't possibly know whether you're pregnant.'

'Of course I can know. I have insight, Michael. You must know that by now. I just know. Like you knew that that artist would be struck by lightning.'

He felt decidedly uncomfortable. He had never mentioned that episode to her. She was reading his mind. He wanted to get out of the room, wanted to go for a long walk in the middle of the night, far from her, far from her thought.

'Why don't you go for a walk? You need some fresh air,' she said.

'Can you also read my mind when I'm not in your presence?'

'I've never tried. But everything is possible if you work at it.'

He slipped on his trousers, his shirt, his shoes. He was only going to go round the block, round the hotel, have a look at the pool, maybe have a swim if there was no one around.

He waved her goodbye and closed the door.

Already the pattern of the carpet in the corridor was comforting, anything reliable was. He went through the double doors out into the patio and sat down on a garden chair.

If he accepted the fact that he was dealing with a supernatural individual, that is a person who had definite psychic powers, he should also accept the idea that she was pregnant.

If so, then he should ask her to have an abortion.

He didn't want a child of his own now, he didn't want one from her, he certainly didn't want a 'superchild' as she was predicting.

He'd ask her point blank to get rid of it.

He sat in the cool of the night a while longer aware now that he found it hard to relax by himself for fear of some oppressive message coming to him either from the past or the future so, restless, he got up and walked back to the hotel room.

Melanie was standing naked in front of the mirror examining her bruises.

'Astral projection?' he asked.

'Not tonight.'

He sat down heavily on the bed.

'Does the mirror help?'

'A lot of it has to do with sex, Michael,' she said getting back into bed. 'The orgasm is a very necessary part of the reproduction process; if you try to reproduce yourself by yourself, a mirror helps.'

'What do you do?'

'I masturbate feverishly, what the hell do you think I do?'

It made him feel uncomfortable.

He wasn't even sure whether she was telling the truth or making fun of him.

'How did you learn all this? Did you have a teacher?'

'Oh yes, Michael, my guru, a very tall, very strong totally bald man with not a hair on his body and with a gigantic penis taught me everything I know. He used to sit cross-legged on a mat and make me lie naked in front of him and watch me play with myself . . . '

240

She was laughing at him.

'You said you couldn't have done it alone. In New York when the lights went out, you said you couldn't have done it alone. What did you mean?'

'Other people are improving on themselves.'

'Many?'

'Lots, I would have thought.'

'But did you know that that night certain people were going to . . . to get together to cause the blackout?'

'Was it planned you mean?'

'Yes.'

'Yes, it was planned.'

'So there's an authority?'

'No. Just three of us.'

'Who are the other two?'

'You can guess.'

He thought, then remembered the other charts, the other family trees.

'Gregoriev and Capuela?'

'Gregoriev and Capuela,' she confirmed. 'But as they are men they can't reproduce themselves as I can. Well, they could if they found another intensely psychic woman who fancied them.'

'Was Sarah as psychic as you?'

'Not quite. But this child will be,' she patted her stomach.

'When is it due?' he asked.

'May third next year.'

It was hard to believe but apparently these super psychics were roaming the world looking for each other to multiply. He was one of them, had been without knowing it. It was like having a rare blood group, but a lot more frightening.

'How long have you been planning to meet me?'

'Years. Since I was fifteen.'

'And you traced me through Sarah?'

'I traced you, got to know Sarah so that I'd get to know you.'

'So it was all carefully plotted in advance?'

'I'm afraid so. But I do actually like you, and you're a very interesting man and fun to be with.'

'Thanks.'

It was lunacy. Maybe she was mad and was making it all up, but Huejelar and Paris and Albacota and everything else he'd been over and over in his mind were not fiction, not inventions; it had all been real like her disappearance and reappearance and the New York black-out.

It was the look in her eyes he mistrusted.

Not once had she said that these powers could do something good for the world. She was power-mad, greedy to get the better of everyone else. If the child was born it would be a monster and he would have to make sure it wasn't born.

'I'm not going to have an abortion, Michael, if that's what you're going to suggest.'

She was reading him again.

'I think we should discuss it, that's all.'

'And I'm not greedy for power for its own sake. I want to shake the world into realizing that there is a fourth dimension, but to do that, because the majority of people are so fast asleep, you have to shock. And shocks come through disasters.'

'Why don't we go back home, to Cagnes, where we can both relax and talk it over? I'm confused. Besides I think we should have confirmation of a pregnancy

243

before we start arguing about whether the child should be born or not. We should at least wait a month.'

'I think we should wait nine,' she said, getting up.

He watched her cross the room, take a cigarette out of the packet on the table, then go into the bathroom.

She closed the door, he heard the catch turn.

He relaxed.

He was going to buy time again, at an unknown cost. It had happened with Norma several times, especially when Sarah had been young; arguments based on little more than a conflict of ideas as to what the future should be. He'd kept quiet, waited, taken the decision he wanted and acted on it and invariably found that she had come round to his point of view, often because it was easier.

Maybe Melanie wasn't like that, but he'd play the same game. To be told that he was going to be the father after a few nights was ridiculous.

He felt like a cigarette, so got up and took one from the packet.

And supposing she was pregnant, just simply pregnant and all that occult rubbish she had hurled at him was, well, rubbish! Would he mind?

Yes.

He didn't want to saddle himself with the responsibility of another child, not in this atmosphere, not with her seeing it as a child of destiny. If she settled down and reverted to being the nice girl she had been before they had started hunting ghosts, then it would be different. But now he longed for the quiet uninvolvement of the simple bachelor life.

He wasn't even sure he wouldn't sell the house and live in a Provençal village. The elevator irritated him, the whole size of the place. A penthouse apartment in Nice overlooking the promenade, maybe, easy to manage, far from the madding crowd yet directly above it.

He didn't want to get married again, though he quite wanted a companion.

What did he want? He didn't know.

He glanced at his watch. She had been in the bathroom for more than twenty minutes.

He crossed the room and knocked gently on the door.

'Melanie?'

No answer.

He knocked louder.

'Melanie?'

He banged on the door, tried the door knob, but it was locked from the inside on a one-sided catch.

'Melanie!'

Two immediate thoughts occurred to him, the first was that she had fainted and needed help, the second he instantly rejected, but only because he feared it.

He pressed himself hard against the door and it did not give at all. He backed away and threw himself against it but it was like a brick wall. He had no desire to break his shoulder.

He studied the door carefully. It opened inwards, the lock was half-way up, its weakest points would be at the top and bottom corners.

He pressed his foot hard against the bottom corner and saw the wood give way a fraction. If he could wedge something in there, it might snap.

He tapped the door all over; it wasn't solid, there seemed to be a centre panel. He looked around the room for something suitably strong. The chair.

He lifted it, and swung it back at hip level, then threw it with all his force at the door. Something cracked.

He did it again, aiming at the same spot. The door cracked. He did it again and again, aware that someone might soon object to the disturbance, but he went on until a large splinter could be eased away. He then threaded his hand through the hole, reached the inside catch and opened the door.

She had gone. This time she had gone physically. There was no cupboard, nowhere to hide. The window was closed from the inside and was too small to get through anyway.

He looked in the bath again. Nothing. No trace of her.

And where would she go? Where would she reappear totally nude where the appearance of a naked human being would not arouse too much suspicion?

He went back into the bedroom,

opened the cupboard and took out one of her dresses. He held it firmly in his hands, went to the bed and lay down.

Relax, relax. Nothing will come in this state of tension.

Godammit! If he was as psychic as she said, he should get some message.

He got up, went to the bathroom and found the little bottle of tranquillizers. He'd really work at this one. He'd find her. She said they would make a team, be able to communicate; well, if he believed her then he should try.

He took one small tablet, went back to the bed, lay down and switched off the light.

Michael closed his eyes and started to relax. The mere thought of having taken a little pill did the trick. It was probably only sugar, but it worked. He started breathing more slowly, made himself go limp. He held the dress to him, laid it out over himself and held it and thought of her, her shape, her hands, her feet, her freckled face, and a number of images came to him in rapid succession.

Big Ben, the Eiffel Tower, the Branden-
burg Gate, the Spanish Steps, the Doges
Palace, Sydney Opera House. He opened
his eyes and shook his head.

This was ridiculous. He could no more
bring on a vision than anyone else. He sat
on the edge of the bed and buried his face
in his hands. Where *would* she go?

Where could a naked person appear
without causing alarm?

A strip show? Another hotel room, a
hospital?

The flash came.

A building, white, modern, low, official,
a flagpole outside, trees, bright blue sky,
heat.

A small hospital?

The image didn't last but he could
work on it. There were cars, large cars
parked outside, it was America, a black
cat, a hearse. A mortuary.

She'd gone to a mortuary, slipped into
one of those filing cabinet-like caskets
and waited for the opportunity to take
someone else's clothes. After that she was
free.

He stood up, stamped his feet and

squeezed his head with both hands.

He was going mad! He was going into the realms of Frankenstein monsters, of horror movies! Yet what had happened to him in the recent past wasn't that far removed from a horror movie. He stayed at the motel for two more days.

He went in and out several times, went for walks, was totally incapable of concentrating on anything, could not sleep without valium.

He reported the damaged door to the management and explained that he had had an agument with his wife who had left him. They were not interested as long as he paid for the repairs. Marital arguments were not uncommon.

He hoped for a telephone call, a message, but nothing came. It was possible, of course, that in her attempt at astral projection something had gone wrong and she had perished. He didn't know how he would react if it was actually confirmed. Deaths of friends and relatives were becoming so much part of his daily life that he would probably just feel relief at being free again.

Deaths and births!

Then it struck him. Why he hadn't thought of it before was incredible. Emma.

Michael picked up the telephone and asked for David's parents' number in England.

He hung up and waited. Lit a cigarette, didn't like the taste. Stubbed it out.

The 'phone rang.

It was Emma's grandmother.

'Just rang up to find out how things were going?' he said.

'Oh Michael, how nice, where are you?'

'In New York,' he lied. Five miles outside Lynchburg would need too much explaining.

'Still? Melanie told us you were going back to Cagnes.'

He was ready for it. He didn't hesitate too long. He saw the whole picture.

'I was delayed, business.'

'We were really expecting her to write to call to say how Emma was, we actually rang there last night.'

'Rang where? Cagnes? And she didn't answer?'

251

'Well, we knew she wasn't there. We were trying to contact *you*.'

Her voice became a little tense, a little piqued. 'It was a very sudden decision . . . we were rather upset.'

'I'm sorry,' Michael stalled. 'What exactly did Melanie do?'

'She just turned up two days ago and said she had to take Emma to the doctor because of her vaccination which had gone wrong. She had a letter to prove it.'

'A letter?'

'Yes, from your doctor in Nice stating that the vaccine they had issued was wrong and that all children had to be taken for treatment at once.'

'How was she dressed?' he asked.

'Dressed? Why?'

'I gave her some money to buy herself new clothes because she always looks so waif-like. I was wondering whether she had done,' he lied.

'Oh . . . she was wearing a sort of Nanny's uniform. We were most impressed. But have you heard from her?'

'Yes, of course. She's in London, and flies home tomorrow.'

He exchanged banalities about the weather, and rang off.

★ ★ ★

Melanie had kidnapped Emma.

She'd blackmail him then, straightforward blackmail until he agreed to her having the baby.

She was banking on him having some feeling for Emma, since she could read his mind she obviously knew he would care, would care more and more as the days went by, would feel more and more responsible, until he gave in.

He would have to tread very carefully with Melanie.

Very carefully indeed.

10

It was obvious he should go home.

From there he would be able to control everything, besides which he was spending a small fortune, staying in hotels.

He drove to Roanoke, took a national flight to La Guardia, an international flight from Kennedy and arrived in Cagnes exhausted some twenty-eight hours later, to find a letter from Melanie postmarked London.

Dear Michael,

Emma and I are well and safe and thank you for your concern. I am going into hiding with her till my baby is born. I will then join you if you want us. Do not worry about us, I can take care of everything. They are both children of destiny.
I love you, father of my child. Melanie.

'I am going into hiding . . . ' He would have to find her. Where would she go, pregnant and with Emma?

He decided to get some sleep. With all the crazy thoughts going through his head, the memories of the last two weeks, two months, the jet lag, he wouldn't be sane enough to make the right decision.

He made himself a cup of tea, left a note for the daily, asking her not to disturb him, and went to bed.

He awoke hungry in the middle of the night, thinking it was nine in the morning. So he got up and went downstairs to the kitchen. He opened the fridge door and found eggs, bacon, fresh milk and fresh fruit in abundance; he cooked himself an English breakfast and ate it heartily.

To start the search for Melanie he would try all the divinatory means at his disposal: clairvoyance through her personal possessions, day dreams, memories, everything. He would turn her room upside down, inside out, till he found something significant.

He went upstairs into the familiar room. Melanie had left most of her things. In the drawer with the charts and the deeds he found a pack of Tarot cards and a book explaining their divinatory meanings.

He knelt down in front of the bed, shuffled the cards, cut them and shuffled them again, then laid out three in a row, face down.

It was so silent he could only hear his own breathing.

As he turned the cards over, one by one, he concentrated hard on Melanie. When he saw her in his mind, as he had seen her nude in the Renoir Garden, he fixed his mind on that image, then looked at the cards.

The Queen of Cups.

The Two of Swords.

The Moon, reversed.

He studied them for a long time, checked the alternative divinatory meanings and came up with a perfect reading.

The Queen of Cups: *Good fair woman, honest, devoted, who will do service to the Querent.*

The Two of Swords: *Tenderness,*

affection, intimacy.
The Moon, reversed: *Instability, inconstancy, silence.*

He was thirsty and felt like a good long drink. He went all the way down to the kitchen and mixed himself a vodka, orange juice and grenadine. He then went out into the garden, down to the lemon trees and picked one of the riper fruit. How glorious to be alone in one's own place and pick lemons off the trees.

He looked up and there was a crescent moon.

Instability, inconstancy, silence. Had he made her unstable?

Tenderness, affection. Maybe he had been very destructive with his suggestion of an abortion. Maybe she needed that child.

Maybe she needed him.

He went back upstairs and returned to the cards, shuffled the pack again, cut it, shuffled it again and placed the top card face down below the three already laid out. Then he turned it over. The Nine of Swords.

He dreaded its divinatory meaning.

Death, failure, miscarriage, delay, deception, disappointment, despair.

Miscarriage.

Despair.

He would have to find her.

He quickly drank down the cocktail, gathered up the cards and lay down on the bed, waiting for the alcohol to take effect.

An image came into his mind quite slowly. First the sea, a rough sea, a grey-green sea, then a promenade, wind-swept, wet with drizzle, a row of seafront terrace houses, pale blue, pink, yellow, desperately competing with the bad weather to make the place more cheerful. Tall hills behind, a figure pushing a pram, holding an umbrella against the wind, then the number '21' on the gate of the house.

He opened his eyes.

'She's in a British seaside resort,' he said aloud, and was surprised at his use of the word 'British.'

Why not English?

'Because she's in Wales,' he said aloud again.

A Welsh seaside resort? How many were there?

He went quickly down to the study and took out all the relevant books from the shelf: guides, maps, travel books.

Porthcawl, Llanelli, Aberystwyth, Llandudno, Colwyn Bay, Rhyl . . .

He would go. He would go to every goddam one. He would fly to London, hire a car, go right round the coast of Wales, start at Newport and work his way round until he got to a place which had vibrations, which told him she was nearby. He was confident he could do it. He had powers, she had said so and now he believed her.

He'd find her.

* * *

The food served for the evening meal in the King's Head Hotel, Llanbrydpool, was appalling. British hotel food was something Michael had forgotten about.

The place was warm and comfortable, rustic with its beams, silent with its thick pile carpets. In the lounge bar the richer locals drank their gins and tonics, in the public bar the poorer drank their pints of tepid beer.

He had stayed one night in London, then driven up the M4 in his hired Ford Granada, chosen partly because of its name, making use of every possible good omen. He'd enjoyed the drive, especially the greenery of the countryside, and now, after the frozen duck a l'orange, and a not very good wine, he went up to bed, having glanced in the television room and decided he wouldn't be able to stand the programme.

He lay back in the double bed in total darkness holding, in one hand, an imitation ivory bracelet Melanie often wore, and in the other, one of Emma's tiny nightdresses, both of which articles he had brought with him for divinatory purposes.

In the moments before sleep he worked on the image of the girl pushing the pram along the sea front.

Like a home-movie, the girl started walking along the pavement and turned up a side street away from the front. She was going shopping, she did this regularly, and he followed her, was right behind her, saw Emma in the pram now, saw Melanie's hands pushing the pram, *was* Melanie.

He passed a launderette, a gift shop, a Chinese restaurant. He could smell the food, the impression was strong, a Chinese take-away and restaurant in Aberystwyth.

Her thoughts, not his.

Aberystwyth.

★   ★   ★

It was a two-and-a-half-hour drive across the Black Mountain. The day was crisp, bright, enjoyable, and not for one moment did Michael have doubts. He had complete confidence in himself, in his extra-sensory powers; he was now learning how to use them.

He reached Aberystwyth at eleven and drove straight to the sea front. The houses were brighter, larger, the atmosphere less cramped than in the vision.

He drove up the main street to check out the Chinese restaurant and there it

261

was, five doors down from the launderette, three doors away from a souvenir giftshop. Incredible.

He drove back to the sea front and parked a little way down from Number 21. It was possible that she had had a forewarning of his arrival and might have left; on the other hand he meant her no harm; on the contrary.

He got out of the car, crossed the road and paused outside the house. A 'Bed and Breakfast' notice was stuck in the front room window. Out of season she would be able to stay there cheaply.

He rang the bell.

The door was opened by an amiable grey-haired lady in a floral dress; behind her in the hall he could see a pram — dark blue, not black, smaller than he had imagined.

'Melanie Forbes?' he asked.

'Melanie Forbes? No there's no one of that name here . . . ' her voice chanted.

She'd changed her name, of course.

'The young lady with the baby?'

'My daughter? Gwyneth? You want to see Gwyneth?'

Gwyneth came out of the front room holding a baby. Mother, daughter and grandchild stared at him with interest.

'I'm sorry, I've made a mistake. There's no one else living here, with a baby?'

'No, only me and my husband and Gwyneth's hubby at present.'

'I must have the wrong address.'

He smiled, bowed slightly and went back to the car, shattered.

How could he have been led to them?

What connection could there possibly be?

Was it a sign of some sort which he did not understand, or an omen for the young girl? A prediction? Of what?

He got into the car and sat behind the wheel feeling drained. All that way for nothing. The inspiration had originally come in Melanie's room. Had he acted too quickly on intuition? Obviously.

So it meant he couldn't trust himself, unless the woman was a medium.

She could be. Aberystwyth had come to mind in the hotel last night, the sheets, something in the bedroom coming from her? A chambermaid, a member of the family, waves and vibrations getting mixed up? He'd picked up on something else. Could he go in and ask? He had to, there had to be some connection, he had felt so positive about it. The girl's husband? Was he away somewhere and in danger? Was she in danger? He had a duty towards these people, but how frightening it would be to have a strange man knocking at the door and blurting out that he was psychic and had been sent to them, but he didn't know why.

Act! Find out! If he didn't find out he'd never trace Melanie.

As he opened the car door he saw her coming along the street. Exactly the same picture, more distinctive, three-dimensional. The same pram, the same coat. He had never seen her leaving the house, he had seen her in the street, passing it. She lived elsewhere.

He waited, then watched her as she stopped and turned towards him.

Hesitation. What should he do?

He was pleased to see her, really pleased to see her. He loved her maybe. Certainly he wanted to be with her.

He got out of the car.

She put the brake on the pram and crossed the road towards him. They fell into each other's arms.

'I had no idea. I had no premonition at all,' she said.

'I'm the one with premonitions.'

They kissed and, as a car came round the corner, moved quickly to the safety of the pavement. He looked into the pram; Emma was asleep, unaware as usual.

'You're coming back with me to Cagnes. It's ridiculous not to.'

'I had no idea,' she repeated, and her joy, her happiness shone from her whole face.

'Have you seen a doctor?' he asked.

'Of course.'

'And?'

'First week in May.'

★　★　★

For four months, nothing.

Melanie was pregnant and this changed her. There was a mutual understanding between them that the recent past, the psychic experiences had been bad, that both knew they were bad and that they were best forgotten.

At least that is how he read it.

He certainly didn't want to talk about it, didn't want to think about it and as she never brought up the subject he left it alone.

Happily, he went back to work, wrote letters, received letters, read the financial papers, rang round the world for advice, not sure whether to start up again seriously or maybe take a whole year off.

Once they got near to talking of the past, of what they had been through, when she cleared up the room she had occupied and put away all her charts in Norma's box room as though that period of her life was over.

The idea of marrying Melanie weighed fairly heavily on his mind, but he decided to wait to see how things developed.

Sometimes he thought she was aware of this inner plan of his and was behaving in an exemplary manner, but then if she could do that what more could he ask? He was aware that after the birth

might change, but he would wait and
.

So they passed the early winter months
ietly, domestically, going to Nice to see
new film, sometimes watching televi-
on, but mostly passing the time in the
enthouse living room reading and
istening to music.

He had to admit, also, that he himself
had changed. The discovery that he was
psychic, that he could see into the future
was much more than fascinating, it was a
power and therefore a responsibility. He
had the feeling sometimes that he was
being guided, that he was not alone, and
that he was being guided by a good
power, possibly to counter-balance an evil
one. But it was just a feeling which he did
not want to dwell on, for the evil power
he would be opposing could only be one
he did not understand.

Then just before Christmas, on a warm
day while Melanie was taking Emma out
for a walk, he took Melanie's pack of
Tarot cards down to the study to do a
reading on himself.

He hadn't planned it, the idea just

came to him and he acted on impu
The problem he couldn't solve was
whether he should marry her, whet
she wanted to be married, whether
could, like his more broadminded c
temporaries, live with her and have her
the unmarried mother of his child.

He did not believe that by the mere
shuffling of a pack of pretty cards he
could foretell the future, but the cards did
jar the mind into realizing, accepting or
negating facts.

If he did not like a card which
suggested he *should* get married, then he
would not do so. He was asking the
pack's advice, advice which might not
necessarily be correct but would help him
make up his mind. It was cheaper than
going to a psychiatrist who would
certainly certify him the moment he
started talking about a future wife who
became transluscent in the night and
could cross the Atlantic in fifteen minutes
to call him up on the 'phone.

He concentrated his thoughts on
Melanie and himself, on marriage, on
their relationship. He shuffled, cut, and

shuffled again, laid three cards down face downwards then turned them up.

They were the same three cards as five months ago before he had gone to get her in Wales.

The Queen of Cups.

The Two of Swords.

The Moon.

Only this time the first two were reversed.

He looked up the divinatory meanings.

The Queen of Cups — reversed: *Perverse woman, not to be trusted.*

The Two of Swords — reversed: *Falsehood, duplicity.*

The Moon: *Danger, deception, occult forces.*

The old fear seeped back into his stomach. She was deceiving him. The pretence at the perfect life was a lie. She was lulling him into a false sense of security, all the time making sure the child would be born.

The charts came to mind. The day she had put the charts away. It had been too pat, too much what he wanted.

He left the study, went up to the box

room where all Melanie's psychic material had been put away in a trunk.

It was strange, but he now realized he hadn't been in Norma's room since that day. Several times he had gone up there to talk to Melanie, but she had always met him on the stairs, or in the corridor outside.

He opened the door. She had changed things round, placed the trunk against the opposite wall, put the sewing machine behind the door, had unrolled an old Indian carpet on the floor and the full-length mirror originally in her room was again leaning lengthwise against the wall so that if she lay on the carpet she could see herself.

He opened the trunk. The famous chart was on top and he unrolled it. She had put in other names since he had last seen it, had connected the lines confirmed by their visit to Huejelar and Paris. At the bottom she had added two new names.

Emanating from a union between himself and herself was the name Adam. Emanating from Adam was a line coupling him with Emma and from that astonishing union a line to a space surrounded by small sunlike rays.

He unrolled all the other charts, went through all the boxes and suitcases in the room, even looking under the carpet and behind the mirror. There was nothing else, just this quite incredible addition to his family chart.

Melanie then foresaw Emma and the new child producing a . . . superior being?

It was hideous, mad, incestuous, perverse . . .

To have this woman in charge of his grandchild, and carrying his own, was lunacy. She was planning twenty years ahead, saw herself as a grandmother superior. And why this feeling that it was evil, that it was really evil?

He needed guidance. Oh, he needed guidance!

He would wait. He would bide his time.

If he was destined to cause her end, to destroy her, if the powers behind him were going to use him for the good, then an opportunity would occur, would be pointed out. He would know what to do.

If it wasn't already too late. If he wasn't losing his sense of reality, losing his mind.

★ ★ ★

In the evening they had got into the habit of eating in the kitchen, then going up to the penthouse sitting-room to watch the news. More often than not he went up first while she finished clearing up and he had never questioned this little domestic routine. She wasn't that interested in the French news and he certainly wasn't interested in washing up, which she claimed she enjoyed.

So, for at least half an hour every night they were not together, the only regular time of the day when they were not.

He said nothing during the meal that evening and went up to the penthouse sitting room as usual, using the elevator. Once at the top, however, after switching on the television, he came slowly down the stairs and stopped to listen.

The footfall was so quiet that he nearly missed it, but he concentrated all his hearing on the corridor leading to the box-room and, unmistakably, he heard a footfall, and the quiet click of the door closing.

Taking off his shoes he padded down, paused outside the door, opened it cautiously and looked in.

Three candles were lit and placed on the floor two feet from the mirror. Between the candles and the mirror Melanie lay, naked, on her left side facing the mirror.

He looked at her reflection which was quite unbelievable. She was more than transluscent, she was partly transparent, and in the area of her stomach he could see the pulsating shape of a foetus.

Her eyes were closed and she was breathing very regularly, very slowly. Then his knees cracked and she turned to look at him.

'You shouldn't have come,' she said sharply.

'What are you doing?'

'The child is to inherit your powers of precognition. From me he is to inherit the powers of astral projection and psychokinesis.'

'Psychokinesis?' He wasn't sure what she meant.

'My poor Michael. You don't know anything, do you? Psychokinesis is the ability to change the fundamental construction of seemingly solid objects, to twist, to bend, to change the direction of, to move objects from one place to another. Remember the lock on the crypt door in Paris? How do you think I opened it? And your car door in Huejelar when I went to get the crutch? I can bend a one-inch thick copper tube just by looking at it. I can even put lights out in cities by paralysing generators.'

There was something so malicious in her expression that he suddenly feared her, hated her.

'Come with me,' she said, getting up and taking his hand.

Nude, she led him down the stairs to their bedroom, opened the window, the outside shutters, and pulled him out onto the balcony. For a moment he was concerned about her catching cold, but then decided that she probably couldn't even feel it.

'Don't worry, Michael, I have inner warmth,' she said, amused, reading his mind. 'Now look down there at the town.' He looked. A mixture of blackness and darkness.

Shadows, orange lights, white lights became sharper as he got accustomed to the night, the blues and greens of the neon signs shone out, the headlamps of cars in the distance spotlighted the façades of the buildings. Fairyland from this viewpoint, civilized fairyland. It made him feel secure.

Then quite suddenly it all went black.

All of it, including the headlamps of the cars.

Within seconds he heard a scream, then another, then the shattering of glass, the crunch of metal, accidents happening in every part of the area.

'It'll last two minutes,' Melanie said icily. 'That is how powerful I am. For now I am working alone.'

He was numb.

In the dark, now broken in small areas by emergency lights, torches in gardens, candles in windows, he listened to her.

'Emma and Adam will start a new era in history, the supernatural age, and eventually in twenty years or so, their offspring will take over. You can be part of it, or not. As you wish.'

The lights went on again.

He didn't know how he was going to do it, but he knew that he had to. He could push her off the terrace, the top terrace, destroy her and the child to come and allow Emma to grow up and live in peace, burn the charts, rid himself of everything connected with her.

'Killing me won't necessarily solve the problem, Michael. Besides, the Quatrain has a message for you.'

Still naked, she led him back into the bedroom and downstairs into the study to take the framed Quatrain off the wall where it had hung since she had given it to him.

'It can be interpreted a different way, you see. *'Near olive trees and nudity by starlight'* . . . You, next to me. *'Parent of the twenty-first, unique on earth.'* You again. Father of this child to be. Calculations can either be made from

Nostradamus himself, or from his first offspring. '*Divine, the mother soon under a veil*' . . . Me. The veil is the astral body. '*Father dead of narrow and deep fall . . .*' a warning I think, Michael, don't you? A warning to you.'

He wasn't sure what to think. He just felt that he was being manipulated, that she could twist anything round to suit herself.

' '*Auprés d'oliviers et nudite etoile . . .*' I've never been sure about that first line, whether etoile meant stars, or 'and canvas' . . . Do you have feelings about it?'

He had no feelings about anything.

'Let's go up on the terrace under the stars and see if we get any feelings.'

Was she going to push him over?

He would be cautious. He would be very careful not to go near the edge.

He opened the elevator gates for her and they both got in.

Though they were lovers, though it was his elevator, his house and though they were alone, because he was dressed and she was completely naked, he felt embarrassed and instinctively stood a little away from her.

'Did you know that man draws invisible circles around himself and the diameter of this area is an indication of his emotional state? The personal space of a well-balanced person is cylindrical and extends about eighteen inches in all directions. Each of us apparently defends this area. The space is much larger however, for persons of a violent disposition.'

The lift stopped.

They were between the third and fourth floors and Melanie was looking at herself in the mirrors.

'What's happened now?' he asked, pushing all the buttons in turn, irritated.

''Father dead of narrow and deep fall . . .'' Melanie quoted.

'It's not a power failure, the lights are still on,' he said, not taking any notice. Then he looked at her.

'What did you say?'

'Père mort d 'une chute étroite et profonde.'

He had felt imminent death once before, in Jaume Lanotte's memory when buried under mud. The fear that started around the heart, dropped strangely to the stomach and rose rapidly, coldly up the spine to the back of the neck; it was with him now.

He reached out and touched her. She was growing paler, her skin was white and as she stood staring at her reflection, her eyes glazed over.

He understood what was going to happen.

'Melanie!'

The sound came with difficulty from his throat.

'Melanie!'

It was near panic.

He grabbed hold of her, shook her, she was like a tailor's dummy, her head lolled down, she went limp and when he let her go she crumbled to the floor in a heap.

She was cold. As cold as if she were dead.

'Melanie?' he said in a loud whisper. 'Please, Melanie, what are you doing?'

''Plaintes et pleurs et hurlements

Traitre de son propre pouvoir et heredité

Son fils née éternellement.
Lui-même mort de perfidité.''
The voice was hollow, but recognizable as hers. It came from above, from the fourth floor.

''Recriminations, tears and hideous screams
Traitor to his own powers and inheritance
His son to be born for eternity
Himself to die of perfidy.''

Michael closed his eyes. Waited for more. She was just showing him what she could do.

'The last quatrain he wrote, Michael, Nostradamus your ancestor. It makes it very clear what has to happen.'

And he heard a metallic noise directly above his head, a tampering with the mechanics of the elevator.

'No, Melanie! For God's sake . . . '

The final noise was that of a small bolt falling a few inches onto the roof of the cage, the whirr of a wheel spinning, sprockets failing to engage, then the systematic snapping of the steel threads of the retaining cable.

He listened to it all, knowing exactly what it was, what it meant, then like a guillotine the cage fell.

He screwed up his eyes, took the impact of the ceiling coming down with upraised arms, was aware for a fraction of a second that he was floating in mid-air, then as the light blacked out he felt the sharp glass splinter of the mirror cut across his throat, blood pulsating out as it cut through the carotid artery, and he heard the cracking of his leg bones as the floor was thrust right up crushing him to death.

There was a brief moment of life left in him, enough to struggle, to protest, to hope . . .

Then he gave up.

THE END

NOSTRADAMUS
DESCENDANCY CHART

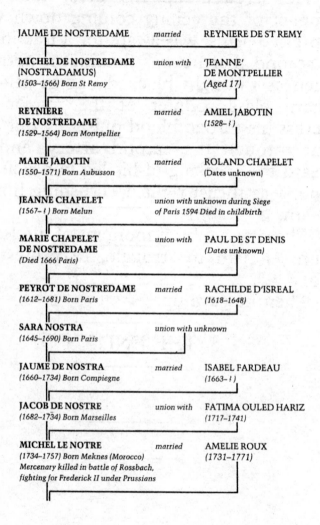

JAUME DE NOSTREDAME	*married*	**REYNIERE DE ST REMY**
MICHEL DE NOSTREDAME (NOSTRADAMUS) *(1503–1566) Born St Remy*	*union with*	**'JEANNE'** **DE MONTPELLIER** *(Aged 17)*
REYNIERE **DE NOSTREDAME** *(1529–1564) Born Montpellier*	*married*	**AMIEL JABOTIN** *(1528–?)*
MARIE JABOTIN *(1550–1571) Born Aubusson*	*married*	**ROLAND CHAPELET** (Dates unknown)
JEANNE CHAPELET *(1567–?) Born Melun*	*union with unknown during Siege* *of Paris 1594 Died in childbirth*	
MARIE CHAPELET **DE NOSTREDAME** *(Died 1666 Paris)*	*union with*	**PAUL DE ST DENIS** *(Dates unknown)*
PEYROT DE NOSTREDAME *(1612–1681) Born Paris*	*married*	**RACHILDE D'ISREAL** *(1618–1648)*
SARA NOSTRA *(1645–1690) Born Paris*	*union with unknown*	
JAUME DE NOSTRA *(1660–1734) Born Compiegne*	*married*	**ISABEL FARDEAU** *(1663–?)*
JACOB DE NOSTRE *(1682–1734) Born Marseilles*	*union with*	**FATIMA OULED HARIZ** *(1717–1741)*
MICHEL LE NOTRE *(1734–1757) Born Meknes (Morocco)* *Mercenary killed in battle of Rossbach,* *fighting for Frederick II under Prussians*	*married*	**AMELIE ROUX** *(1731–1771)*

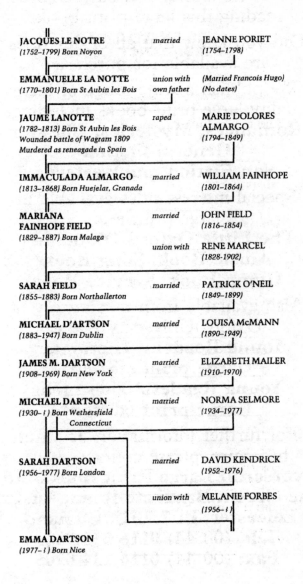

JACQUES LE NOTRE
(1752–1799) Born Noyon

married

JEANNE PORIET
(1754–1798)

EMMANUELLE LA NOTTE
(1770–1801) Born St Aubin les Bois

union with
own father

(Married Francois Hugo)
(No dates)

JAUME LANOTTE
(1782–1813) Born St Aubin les Bois
Wounded battle of Wagram 1809
Murdered as reneagade in Spain

raped

MARIE DOLORES
ALMARGO
(1794–1849)

IMMACULADA ALMARGO
(1813–1868) Born Huejelar, Granada

married

WILLIAM FAINHOPE
(1801–1864)

MARIANA
FAINHOPE FIELD
(1829–1887) Born Malaga

married

JOHN FIELD
(1816–1854)

union with

RENE MARCEL
(1828-1902)

SARAH FIELD
(1855–1883) Born Northallerton

married

PATRICK O'NEIL
(1849–1899)

MICHAEL D'ARTSON
(1883–1947) Born Dublin

married

LOUISA McMANN
(1890–1949)

JAMES M. DARTSON
(1908–1969) Born New York

married

ELIZABETH MAILER
(1910–1970)

MICHAEL DARTSON
(1930–?) Born Wethersfield
            Connecticut

married

NORMA SELMORE
(1934–1977)

SARAH DARTSON
(1956–1977) Born London

married

DAVID KENDRICK
(1952–1976)

union with

MELANIE FORBES
(1956–?)

EMMA DARTSON
(1977–?) Born Nice

We do hope that you have enjoyed reading this large print book.

Did you know that all of our titles are available for purchase?

We publish a wide range of high quality large print books including:
Romances, Mysteries, Classics
General Fiction
Non Fiction and Westerns

Special interest titles available in large print are:
The Little Oxford Dictionary
Music Book, Song Book
Hymn Book, Service Book

Also available from us courtesy of Oxford University Press:
Young Readers' Dictionary
(large print edition)
Young Readers' Thesaurus
(large print edition)

For further information or a free brochure, please contact us at:
Ulverscroft Large Print Books Ltd.,
The Green, Bradgate Road, Anstey,
Leicester, LE7 7FU, England.
Tel: (00 44) **0116 236 4325**
Fax: (00 44) **0116 234 0205**

Other titles in the
Linford Mystery Library:

PROJECT JOVE

John Glasby

Norbert Donner and Project Director Stanton work on Project Jove, observing the robots in the Jupiter surface lab by means of the Fly, a remote-controlled exploratory ship. Then Senator Clinton Durant arrives from earth convinced Stanton is hiding something on Jupiter's surface. And, unconvinced of dire warnings of danger, he and his assistants ride a Fly down to question the surface lab robots. They soon find themselves completely at the mercy of the giant planet and its devastating storms . . .

THE STELLAR LEGION

E. C. Tubb

Wilson, a waif of the war of unity, spends his boyhood in forced labour. When he is sent to the penal world of Stellar, he survives, winning promotion in the Stellar Legion, a brutal military system. Laurance, Director of the Federation of Man, wants to dissolve the Legion. He pits his wits against its commander, Hogarth. He's terrified lest the human wolves, trained and hardened in blood and terror, should ravage the defenceless galaxy . . .

ENDLESS DAY

John Russell Fearn

It's June 30th. And in Annex 10, situated in the Adirondack Mountains of New York, scientist Dr. Gray and his team can hardly believe their instrument readings. It's four o'clock, and as the seconds pass, they see that chaos looms for mankind. The Earth is growing hotter, temperatures rocket, as the sun shines through the night and causes endless days. Everyone suffers — the rich, the poor, the criminal and the family man. Will it ever end?

EIGHT WEIRD TALES

Rafe McGregor

A curious woman investigates the dark secrets harboured within the ancient chapel of a ruined signal station. An antique ivory hunting horn will spell the downfall of Professor Goodspeed. Meanwhile, an eldritch voice draws a lonely man ever closer to the drowned town of Lod . . . Eight short tales, each directly inspired by a master of the mysterious or supernatural — Arthur Conan Doyle, H.P. Lovecraft, Anthony Hope, or M.R. James — which will send chills down your spine . . .